Getting in the Game

DAWN FITZGERALD

ACKNOWLEDGMENTS

In loving appreciation for my family and first readers, John, Ryan, and Brynn. Thank you, Mom and Dad, for cheering me on through hundreds of soccer games and track meets. My brother, Sean, thank you for sharing your stories and reading mine. Tim FitzGerald, Jack McGuane, and John Malloy, thank you for sharing your hockey expertise. Kristen Bettcher, Ben Tomek, Don Gallo, and the Solon Library Children's Writers Group, thank you for your support and encouragement. Diana Leitch and Chris and Maureen De Vito, thank you for standing up for a girl's right to compete in any sport. Deborah Brodie, I will always be grateful for your generous invitation to get in the game!

SQUARE
FISH

An Imprint of Holtzbrinck Publishers

Library of Congress Cataloging-in-Publication Data
FitzGerald, Dawn.
Getting in the game / Dawn FitzGerald.—1st ed.
p. cm.
"A Deborah Brodie book."
Summary: When everyone tries to get thirteen-year-old Joanna off the boys' ice hockey team, including Ben, her best friend since kindergarten, Jo resolves to deal with the problems caused by her participation.
[1. Hockey—Fiction.   2. Best friends—Fiction.   3. Sex role—Fiction.   4. Determination (Personality trait)—Fiction.   5. Family problems—Fiction.   6. Middle schools—Fiction.   7. Schools—Fiction.   8. Ohio—Fiction.]   I. Title.
PZ7.F572Ge 2005   [Fic]—22   2004017547

ISBN-13: 978-0-312-37753-3 / ISBN-10: 0-312-37753-3

Originally published in the United States by Roaring Brook Press
Book design by Jennifer Browne
Square Fish logo designed by Filomena Tuosto
First Square Fish Edition: January 2008
10 9 8 7 6 5 4 3 2 1
www.squarefishbooks.com

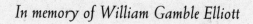

In memory of William Gamble Elliott

One

I must have hit my head pretty hard when I fell and bit my lip, because I remember thinking that it didn't look like blood on the ice—at least not mine. More like a snow cone or slushy with Bahama-Mama flavored syrup. My next thought—if my name were Ashley or Brittany, I wouldn't be in this mess—only proved that Derek knocked the crap out of me when he cheap-shotted me into the boards.

A girl named Brittany or Ashley would have fallen in love with the spandex costumes and the white skates of a figure skater. But when your name is Joanna, and everyone calls you Jo, you grow up in Cleveland watching your older brother play ice hockey in the shadow of the steel mills and dream of the day when you can wear a jersey and carry a stick, waiting for your chance to slap that puck home.

For years, I settled for dressing up in my brother Jim's hockey uniform for Halloween. It didn't bother me that it was five sizes too big, or that most girls my age were ballerinas and brides. I just wanted to get in the game. I even made my mom blacken my front teeth for that authentic NHL look.

As soon as I was old enough, I skated with the boys and a few other girls in youth hockey leagues. Every year, a girl dropped out. Some switched to figure skating, most joined soccer, basketball, or cheerleading. Eventually, everyone learned their place.

Until one day I was the only girl left. Maybe I'm a slow learner, or really stubborn, because I refuse to give up or let Derek intimidate me and ruin my chances by knocking me on my butt during tryouts for our middle school hockey team.

I don't care that I'm the only girl out here, or the smallest player. I don't care that some people think I shouldn't be here. But I *do* care that the drills have stopped and my potential teammates are staring at me now like I'm roadkill.

Coach Granato skates over and checks my lip. "Joanna, why don't you take it easy and hit the locker room for today?"

He doesn't know me very well. I never take anything easy and I'd rather kiss Derek's padded butt than leave the ice right now with everyone thinking it's too rough out here for a seventh-grade girl. Everyone, that is, except Ben.

Ben McCloud and I have been friends ever since his family moved in across the street the summer before kindergarten. I remember sitting on the curb watching the movers sweat all over the McCloud furniture as they hauled it from the truck, heaved it into the house, and dropped each piece with a terrific crash. Mr. McCloud paced around, cursing at everyone to be more careful.

A skinny redheaded kid looked both ways and then double-checked again before crossing the street. He had a shy smile and a bazillion freckles. He stood there staring at me as I poked a stick into a pink glob of chewed bubble gum baking on the hot asphalt road.

"Want some?" I asked, as I stretched the gum in two and offered him half.

He popped it into his mouth, gravel grits and all. We've been best friends ever since.

But right now Ben looks confused. One minute he's giving me a look that says, "Get off the ice. Save yourself!" and the next he's glaring at Derek like he's going to sucker punch him.

Derek doesn't look worried, though. Unlike most hockey players, Ben's not a fighter. Like Gretsky, he uses his skill to avoid conflict on and off the ice.

Instead, Ben offers me his hand, helping me toward the locker rooms, as Coach suggested. He almost trips when I dig in my blades.

"I'm okay, Coach." I grip my stick. "Bit my lip, that's all." I leave out the fact that I'm seeing double and my legs feel like straw.

Coach Granato gives me a hard look, probably debating whether he should cut me from the team right then and there. "All right then, let's move it!" he shouts. "Two lines for shooting drills."

I skate to the closest line, my vision clearing and legs kicking into autopilot. Ben interrupts my revenge fantasy.

"Jo, are you crazy?" he asks.

I blink and stare at him for a second. Good sign, only one Ben standing there. I'll make it through this practice.

"What?" I skate ahead of him, hoping he'll play along and pretend he didn't see me get decked back there.

One problem, though—he did. Everyone did.

"Derek doesn't want you on this team," Ben says to the back of my head. "He's going to do everything he can to make you look bad." He grabs my jersey and pulls me around to face him. "Are you listening? I heard him talking in the locker room before practice."

"Whoa! News flash." I surprise myself with how unconcerned I sound, when every part of me is fighting the urge to retreat into the girls' bathroom, where I can bawl my eyes out and read any new graffiti written on the stall doors.

Maybe it's the taste of blood in my mouth, or how angry I am at Derek, but I turn to Ben, slapping my stick on the ice. "Screw him," I say. "I'm making this team."

He shakes his head, looking even more worried. "That's not the point, Jo."

I give his helmet a quick rap with my glove and hold my stick like a microphone, announcing, "Jo Giordano, the coolest chick on ice, takes 'em all on. Blinds 'em with her speed. Dazzles 'em with her fancy stick work." I give a quick shoulder fake. "Blows 'em away with her amazing passes!"

Ben's not buying it. He shoves me. "Cut the crap!"

I laugh and shrug.

Coach's whistle pierces the arena, and the solid *crack* of the puck striking the tempered glass reminds us why we're out here.

Ben lowers his voice and says, "Be careful, okay? Watch your back."

I smile. "You watch it! I'm playing hockey." Ben groans and skates away to the opposite line.

I take a deep breath, trying to ignore the throbbing pain in my lip and the fear rising in my gut, but I've made my choice. Nothing else I can do now but dig in, tense my muscles, and beat the other guy to the puck the second Coach shouts, "Go!"

Two

"**J**oanna Giordano?" My homeroom teacher waves a pink slip in the air. "Principal's office."

Immediately, I run through a mental checklist: got my lunch, didn't cut any classes, no recent trouble with teachers or cafeteria ladies.

Then Valerie Holm, queen of the seventh grade, announces, "I bet Mr. Lubic wants to run a DNA test to see if Jo's allowed to try out for the boys' hockey team."

Everyone laughs, most from relief that Valerie has chosen her prey this morning—me! The queen bee and her drones thrive on inflicting humiliation and pain five days a week, eight hours a day, with time off for holidays and summer vacation.

Usually, I avoid them by sitting in the back of the room and not calling attention to myself. Besides cutting remarks now and then about my long, curly hair, which I refuse to have chemically straightened, or lack of designer clothes, they ignore me.

I turn to Valerie and say, "At least my DNA would test human."

Big mistake.

A chorus of "Dis, dissed ..." echoes around us. So seldom

5

does anyone challenge the queen. Valerie laughs, casually tossing her streaked hair over her shoulders. But I catch a flicker of surprise and then fury in her eyes because I didn't take the cut and scurry out of the room like the nobody she thinks I am.

Her cloned friends, Heather and Courtney, go into attack mode. "Bitch," Heather says. "No wait, that's insulting to canines."

"Doesn't she look like a sheepdog with that hair?" Courtney asks.

"Hmm, more like a cross between a Labrador and a poodle. A definite Labradoodle," Heather replies.

I don't hang around while they debate the topic. Besides, my Italian grandmother used to say that, with my face and hair, I resemble the girls in Pre-Raphaelite paintings, whatever that means. At least I know I'm no dog.

By the time I reach the door, they're ripping on my father's pickup truck and the nursing home uniform somebody saw my mom wear into the grocery store after work.

"What were you thinking?" I ask myself out loud as I walk down the empty hallway to the office.

Now, I'll deal with Derek on the ice and Valerie off. At least in the rink, I carry a stick and have pads and a helmet for protection. I'm pretty sure that Valerie's attacks will make me look forward to Derek's cheap hits against the boards.

The principal's office is located at the front of the school, near the main doors, which are locked now for everyone's protection. Personally, I'm more worried about what's roaming the halls inside our school than any threat from the outside. Metal detectors, surveillance cameras, and security guards carrying walkie-talkies and pepper spray make it feel like we're doing hard time in here with no chance of parole.

At the office, Principal Lubic is giving instructions to the secretary on today's lockdown code. When he sees me, he points to an open door opposite the copy machine. "Take a seat in my office, Hannah."

Hannah? I shrug and walk in.

In the corner is an old-fashioned red popcorn machine standing on metal wheels with long spokes. It looks like the popcorn machines I saw at carnivals when I was a kid. It doesn't fool me a bit.

The entire wall behind his desk is covered with awards, college degrees, and pictures of Lubic in ugly pants standing on palm-tree-lined golf courses. The only palm tree I've seen in person is the three-inch plastic kind that sticks out of a dinky island in my pet turtle's pool.

A framed certificate states that he holds a doctoral degree in education. I picture Lubic moonlighting on weekends at the emergency room, checking hall passes and scolding nurses: "Move along or you'll be serving a detention!"

Before I finish reading the wall of fame, Lubic strides in and sits down behind a bare glass-topped desk. Not a pen or paper clip, not even dust, interferes with his reflection on the surface.

"Have a seat," he gestures to a chair in front of him. "You're probably wondering, Hannah, why I've called you here this morning."

My heart skips, hoping there's been a mistake and he's got the wrong kid. "I'm Joanna Giordano," I say.

"That's right—Joanna." He leans back slightly in his leather chair and sighs. Then he tells me, "I've received a few phone calls from parents whose sons are trying out for the boys' hockey team here at school."

My stomach knots. He's got the right kid, all right.

"And I've talked to Coach Granato about this situation," he continues.

I stare at his tan hands. Clear nail polish on the nails? I hide my chewed fingernails in my lap, remembering a mouse my father once caught in our basement. It had tried to gnaw off its paws to escape the trap.

"We were thinking that it would be in everyone's best interest if you joined a girls' hockey team, or put your athletic talent to use at figure skating or some other sport this winter."

"Figure skating?" I say, in the same tone I'd use for words like "body odor," "nose hair," and "navel lint."

Lubic gets the message and goes straight to Plan B. "Let's face it, Miss Giordano, a pretty girl like yourself risks getting hurt out there playing with the boys. There're safety concerns we need to consider."

I begin to protest, but he says, "I know"—holding his hand up like a school crossing guard—"Coach says you're a terrific skater, but there's another issue as well. If you made the team, you'd be taking a position that would have gone to a boy."

I stand up, my entire body trembling. "Then let him try

figure skating. I play hockey and there's no girls' hockey team in this town."

A rash flares around Lubic's neck and creeps up the side of his face, but I can't stop myself. "The U.S. women's hockey team won an Olympic gold and silver. Colleges have girls' hockey—Ohio State, Cornell, Boston ..."

He shakes his head. "I understand that, but—"

"Princeton, Harvard, Yale—"

"Young lady!" he barks, pointing his finger in my direction.

"Dartmouth!" I sit down. Why do they always try to control us with *young lady?*

I glance at an engraved plaque on the wall behind his head that reads, DON'T FORGET THE *PAL* IN *PRINCIPAL!*

Yeah, right. *Don't forget the* dic-k *in* dictator.

"Think about it. I know you'll make the smart choice when you consider..." Lubic drones on and on, as if by hearing himself repeat it enough, he can actually convince me that: (a) he's a reasonable and fair guy, looking out for everyone's best interests, and (b) he actually believes that there's a choice to be made and that I have the right to make it.

I daydream during his concerned-principal speech and picture a miniature me in hockey skates etching deep grooves into his glass desktop. Hey, he wants figure skating? I throw in a double axel or two and really do some damage.

He realizes he's lost me, and besides, the law's on my side. He abruptly stands, indicating the meeting's over, with a curt, "Any questions, Miss Giordano?"

I don't think he'll slam me into the boards like Derek, or

make every school day miserable like Valerie, so of the three, Lubic and his Ice Capades fantasy ranks dead last on my list of worries right now.

"Yeah—one." I risk a quick sideways glance at the corner of the room.

He nods expectantly, granting permission.

"That popcorn machine over there work?"

"No," he says in a clipped voice, "it's an antique."

He leaves out "you smart ass," which, when I think about it, shows a lot of control on his part

When I get home that afternoon, the strong smell of garlic hits me as soon as I open the front door, and I know Gramps and my little brother, Michael, are on the loose again in the kitchen. Dangerous combination. Mom's been working a lot of overtime since she asked Dad to move out almost a year ago. They're not divorced or anything, just separated.

Gramps moved in after my older brother, Jim, left for college this fall. About a year ago, Gramps started acting weird—forgetting the names of everyday objects, wearing three or four layers of clothing when he went for his daily walks.

"Don't worry," I told Mom, "the layered look's in."

"Not when it's shorts and T-shirts in January and winter coats on the Fourth of July," she said.

Then there was that incident with crabby Mrs. Stritch, Gramps's old neighbor, who complained that Gramps was talking to her garden statues. She has about fifty of them in her yard: pink flamingos, bullfrogs, full-sized deer, gnomes, and a plastic goose that she keeps on her front porch and dresses in tiny costumes depending on the holiday or the weather.

The goose wears a little yellow rain slicker during thunderstorms; a witch's hat, cape, and broom for Halloween; and pink rabbit ears on Easter. If you ask me, Mrs. Stritch's the crazy one, but she insisted that Gramps was stalking the goose.

One morning, the goose goes AWOL, and Mrs. Stritch calls the police, accusing Gramps of goose-napping. It even made the local paper under the headline FOWL PLAY SUSPECTED FOR MOTHER GOOSE.

Unfortunately, when the police show up at Gramps's front door, the missing goose and two cups of tea are sitting on top of his kitchen table. After the tea party, Gramps came to live with us for good. It's hard on Mom, though, a nurse's aide at a nursing home, taking care of old people all day and then coming home to Gramps, who lately has been having trouble remembering our names.

"What's for dinner?" I ask, giving Gramps a kiss on his scratchy white beard.

Michael's busy stirring what looks like a pot of boiling oatmeal and barely looks up. Gramps stands beside him, still dressed in his pajamas at 6 P.M., smashing something with a rolling pin.

He smiles and says, "Good morning, dear," as he gently brushes my cheek with his hand, which smells like garlic. I give his fingers a quick kiss before letting go.

11

"Like our big pot of humongous secret recipe?" Michael asks as they begin to toss the crushed garlic cloves, one by one, into the cementlike mixture.

"Hmm, looks yummy," I lie.

Dried prunes and a can of green beans are lined up on the counter awaiting the pot. If I nuke the milk tonight before pouring it over a bowl of cereal, can I count it as a hot meal?

The thought of cereal again for dinner makes me want to cry, or scream. I guess it's just everything going on with hockey, school, and worry over Gramps. I'm afraid he's going crazy and I already deal with one crazy man in my life—my father. Though to be fair to Gramps, Dad's crazed in a totally different way.

My dad's been kicked out of so many different things it's hard for me to keep track. Expelled from school numerous times when he was a kid, laid off from his welding job at LTV Steel, ejected from his kids' sporting events. You could say he has a problem with authority figures—especially the kind that wear black-and-white stripes and carry a whistle.

"You gotta let the referee know when he makes bad calls," he tells me every time I'd beg him to be silent during my softball and hockey games.

"What? I'm not allowed to cheer for my daughter?" he demands.

The problem with Dad is that what starts out as "Go team!" ends up as "Are you freakin' blind? Do I hafta come out there, you dumb ref, and show you how to call a game?"

It gets worse.

This past summer, during my championship fast-pitch softball game, the score was tied, 2-2, bottom of the sixth.

12

The opposing team had a runner on third, two outs. I'm on the mound pitching, and all I want to do is strike the batter out so we can end the inning without a run scoring.

But the runner goes to steal home. So I throw the ball to my catcher and she tries for the tag at the plate.

"Safe!" calls the ump.

Immediately, my dad leaps to his feet in the stands, screaming horrible words that basically let the ump and everyone within a mile of the field know that he's not happy with the call.

I want to dig a hole under the pitcher's mound and crawl into it.

Dad runs up to the metal backstop, grabbing it with his hands and shaking it, as he continues verbally abusing the ump, who has turned his back in an attempt to ignore the crazed parent.

Unfortunately, this only enrages Dad more and he's practically scaling the fence to get the ump's attention, but the umpire's had enough.

"You're outta here!" he shouts, giving Dad the arm and ejecting him from the game.

Dad refuses to leave.

By this time, I'm somewhere out in left field desperately searching for a four-leaf clover so I can wish my father off the planet.

Even my teammates' parents beg Dad to calm down and leave because the ump is standing at home plate, arms crossed, refusing to continue the game until my maniac father departs.

When I reach the home run fence, I feel like I'm going to

puke. The weeds are so high out here that I almost convince myself that if I lie down, I'll disappear.

I hear the announcer, Mr. Krumper, a neighbor whose daughter plays first base, shouting over the loudspeaker, "For God's sake, Giordano, leave so we can finish the game!"

A few people in the stands clap. A couple of my teammates do, too, and for a second, I think Mr. Krumper's telling me to leave, until my coach shouts, "Jo, get back on the mound!"

Dad eventually peels out of the parking lot in his pickup, kicking up a cloud of dust and debris and cursing out the window.

"Play ball!" bellows the ump.

My hands shake and a trickle of sweat snakes its way down the back of my neck and in between my shoulder blades. The only way I can finish the inning is to pretend that the lunatic who has just left is in no way related to me.

I refuse to hear the whispering or see the disgusted looks on the parents' faces in the bleachers. I definitely don't hear my friend Taryn, on second base, say to the shortstop, "That's nothing. You should've seen when Jo's mom threw him out of the house."

We lost the championship game that day, 3-2.

Dad didn't come around for two weeks after that scene, which was fine with me. When I see him next, it's at Michael's T-ball game. He's sitting up in the stands, looking harmless and casual in his faded jeans and work boots.

I worry that Dad won't be able to control himself, even with little kids who step up to the tee, swing the bat five times before popping the ball two feet in front of them, and then take off, running straight for third base. I picture Dad shouting, "Hey, somebody get that kid a map!"

During the game, he turns to me and asks, "Plan on trying out for your school's hockey team this winter?"

I'm tempted to lie. I want to tell him, "No way am I trying out for hockey," then I'd never have to see his face in the arena if I made the team. Never have to worry how he might lose control and embarrass me.

I love hockey too much to give it up. Besides, I'm a terrible liar. So I settle for a chilly, "Maybe," figuring what's the use, he'd find out eventually if I made the team.

In dad-speak, "maybe" means "yes!"

"That's my champ," he says, and he puts his arm around my shoulder and kisses my forehead. He looks so pleased sitting there with that dopey proud-parent grin on his face that I almost forgive him. Is it normal to love and hate your dad at the same time?

At that moment, Michael is squatting in right field, studying bumblebees hovering from clover to clover, oblivious to the pop fly sailing his way. The ball falls short, landing a few feet in front of him.

Dad, big smile on his face, stands up and shouts, "Great! I've got myself a botanist, not a ballplayer!"

My cheeks burn and I grip the edge of the metal bleachers with both hands, waiting. My dad should come with a warning label on his T-shirt: CAUTION! FANATIC—PRONE TO UNREASONABLE OUTBURSTS OF FRENZIED ENTHUSIASM DURING SPORTING EVENTS.

But, hell, in a city where football fans dress up as dogs and toss beer bottles at people's heads for fun, maybe Dad's in the "normal" range after all.

He sits back down, chuckling and shaking his head, while everyone around us just laughs—everyone except me.

They probably think Dad's just an easygoing parent, joking about his preschooler's first competitive sports experience. They obviously have no idea who they're encouraging.

How am I ever going to stop him?

Three

When I step out onto the rink for practice, on the third day of tryouts, I can almost see my reflection in the mirrorlike ice. I breathe in the brine-and-ammonia smell and feel hopeful that it's a new beginning. Anything can happen.

Mercury lights, caged in protective steel webs, hang from the high ceiling above and slowly flicker on as Coach announces, "I'll be making cuts and will post the names of the people who have made the team on the locker room door Friday morning."

"Which locker room?" Derek asks. "Boys or girls?"

His friends smirk and elbow him in the back.

I glance over at Ben, but he quickly looks the other way.

Ignoring them, Coach Granato runs his hands through his salt-and-pepper hair and divides us into four lines for a scrimmage. "I'll be trying out some different line combinations today, testing to see who works best with one another. Tough schedule this season. Opening game is in one week against last year's league champs."

I'm psyched that Ben and I are on the same offensive line

and we'll skate together. Because we know each other so well, it'll give both of us a chance to show our strengths.

"Open in the middle!" Coach yells, as I move the puck out of our zone and flick it off my stick to Ben. He takes the shot. It's blocked, but he slams the rebound into the net, hitting the pipes with a satisfying ring.

"Great finish, McCloud. Nice pass, Giordano," Coach calls.

Derek skates by and mimics, "Nice pass, Giordano!"

I ignore him. I'm happy for Ben and that anxious feeling in the pit of my stomach begins to fade away.

It gets even better.

Ben drills another goal and I end up with a goal and two assists. I'm so confident now that we'll both make the team that I blow it during the last five minutes of practice.

Normally, one-on-one drills are my favorite. It's a chance to go head-to-head and show speed and stick skills. But as we line up, I look across to see who I'm up against and my heart skips a beat—Derek!

The whistle blows and we take off after the puck that's skimming along the ice about ten feet in front of us. Derek's a powerful skater and probably outweighs me by fifty pounds, so it's no surprise that he reaches the puck first and takes control.

Battling hard, I get my stick in there and steal it away. Now I'm on offense and Derek's supposed to play defense.

Only, he doesn't.

After I nail my shot and it sails into the back of the net, I realize Derek's not beside me and hasn't even bothered to defend against my scoring. He's already up ahead, skating back to the end of the line.

I skate hard to catch up. Cutting him off in a spray of ice, I say, "You let up!"

With a disgusted look, he spits and pushes me aside, "Get out of my face," he says.

"No!" Before I can stop myself, I slash my stick hard across the backs of his legs.

"What the?" Derek yells and spins around to confront me.

I brace for the blow, but it never comes.

"Derek! Joanna!" growls Coach Granato. "Knock it off and get back in line or you're both finished."

Derek shoves his glove into my jersey. "You're finished," he says, and then skates away.

My legs shake and my throat feels like sandpaper. He doesn't think I'm worth defending against in the drills. He thinks I'm not going to make the team.

Any hockey player would've beaten the crap out of someone for purposely slashing at his legs. He doesn't even think I'm worth fighting!

Somehow, this totally depresses me.

We finish up running the drills and coach says, "Jo, I need to talk to you after practice. The rest of you, I'll see tomorrow."

Ben skates over, looking anxious and pale. "I'll wait for you to walk home," he says to me.

When I step out of Coach's office half an hour later, Ben is sitting on the floor in the hallway, with his back leaning against the gray lockers, working on his homework.

I don't want to talk to anyone and I definitely don't want Ben to see my eyes all red and puffy from crying. He'll think

I'm acting like a typical girl. Hey, can't a person cry when she feels like it? My brother Jim cried whenever we watched *E.T.*, and no one was tougher than Jim on, or off, the ice.

"What happened?" Ben scrambles to throw all his books into his backpack and gather his hockey gear. "Did he cut you from the team?"

"No, not yet. Coach and Lubic probably hope I'll quit first and save them the trouble." I don't wait for Ben to collect his stuff, but keep right on walking toward the exit doors.

"Hey, slow down." He jogs after me. "If he didn't cut you, Jo, that's good. You had a good tryout today."

"Yeah, sure, I showed him. Coach said I'm a strong skater, aggressive, good stick skills, but he also said that having a girl on the team might affect team chemistry." My voice starts to quiver and I can barely get out the last line. "Like the problems I'm having with Derek."

Ben shifts his backpack and gear uncomfortably from one shoulder to the other, and asks, "What did you say?"

"That it's Derek's problem, not mine! Team chemistry? It's hockey, not science lab."

"Maybe he's only trying to help," Ben offers.

"What?" I stop walking and glare at him. "Whose side are you on?"

"Yours, but"—Ben sets his stuff down on the sidewalk and fumbles with the zipper on his jacket—"it's true that some guys don't like having a girl on the team," he says quietly. "Derek's not the only one."

"Why?" I ask, feeling my throat tighten and the tears well up in my eyes again.

"Well, for one thing . . . when you beat us." Ben gives me

a sheepish smile. "I mean, it's wrong, but when I was a kid, my dad used to yell at me, 'Don't throw like a girl, don't skate like a girl, don't run like a girl.'" Ben puts his hand on my arm. "'Quit crying like a girl.'"

I push him away. "Yeah? Well, your dad forgot one, Ben—don't be friends with a girl." I take off so fast that I'm practically racewalking down the icy sidewalk, brushing tears off my face with my mittens.

"Actually," Ben calls after me, "he said that one, too—but I didn't listen!" He catches up, bumping his shoulder into mine.

I pull away.

"Besides, Jo, you're not like a girl, or a boy, to me. You're you—you're just Jo."

"Shut up, McCloud!" I shove him so hard he nearly spills his backpack and gear all over the sidewalk.

Everything's so confusing. I know Ben's just trying to be honest, so why do I feel like pushing him away? All I want is to play hockey—big deal! There're kids at school who smoke, do drugs, have boy/girl sleepovers when their parents are out of town, and have done a lot worse than trying out for a sports team.

We walk in silence the rest of the way home, avoiding patches of ice and each other. I kick at some dirty snow mounds and feel like a raging bull with steam from my breath coming out of my mouth and nose. The streetlights flicker on when we finally stop in front of Ben's house.

"Don't be angry," he says.

But I am angry and mean, and so I cross the street to my house without even saying good-bye.

"Jo, come on," Ben calls after me.

I stand on the uneven sidewalk, back turned toward him, and shout over my shoulder, "I'm moving out of this dumb town, you know."

"Yeah, where to?" he says.

"Canada." From the corner of my eye, I see him struggling not to smile.

"Why Canada, Jo?"

"Because, in Canada, I bet even the Ashleys and the Brittanys play hockey with the boys."

He snorts and shakes his head.

"And kick their butts, too!" I leave Ben standing there and stomp up my porch steps, letting myself in and slamming the door so hard that I knock the stupid wreath off the hook.

The next day at school, Taryn informs me, "They're taking bets."

I shoulder-check my locker to force it open before the bell rings. It gets jammed at least once a day, making me late for class.

"What bets?" The door pops open and I quickly move my knee to block the avalanche of books, sweatshirts, and junk food wrappers tumbling out of the narrow metal opening.

"On whether you make the team or not," Taryn says. "You'll make it, right?"

I shrug, searching for my English book and remembering my talk with Coach yesterday afternoon. "I hope so," I say, but I don't sound very confident.

"Come on, Jo, you will. Besides, I've got two dollars down

on you," Taryn says, tucking her glossy black hair behind her triple-pierced ears.

"Thanks." I find the book under the pile at my feet. "I'll know tomorrow morning. Coach is posting the names."

"Hey, have you considered feng shui for this locker?" Taryn asks, critically surveying the mess.

"No, I hit it here and it usually opens."

She laughs. "Jo, feng shui. Say it like this: *fung shway*."

"Fung shay," I say, feeling like my mouth is full of Novocain.

"Close enough." Taryn kneels down and sorts through the clutter. "It's the Chinese art of positive organization, and right now, you're a mess, girl. My mom runs a consulting business that helps people arrange their stuff so it brings them success and good luck."

"Forget luck," I say. "Help me shove this junk back in or I'll be late for English."

Together we scoop up highlighters, notebooks, and gum wrappers and cram them all back into the locker, but Taryn's found a project. "First, I'll paint the inside of your locker red in order to channel positive chi. Next I'll get some stones and place them along the bottom for—"

"Stones? It's a locker, Taryn, not landscape design!"

The bell rings, drowning out Taryn's miracle makeover plans.

"I'm late!" I slam the door closed—*bang!* And give it a quick kick for good measure.

"Fung this!" I say as we laugh and race off to class.

✳✳✳

23

We're reading the play *Julius Caesar* in English and Ms. Freeman assigns parts that she wants us to perform in front of the sixth graders. I slump down in my seat, hoping to avoid eye contact and a role in the play.

Of course, Valerie's hand is up. She's laughing and calling, "Me, Caesar, me!"

I wonder if she has any idea that Caesar was stabbed to death. I smile, because around here, it's usually Valerie who does all the backstabbing.

Valerie catches my grin and says, "What are you smirking at?"

"Nothing," I mumble, and look down at my book, hoping the no-eye-contact routine works for Valerie as well.

No way.

"So Jo, is it true that you change in the boys' locker room now so you can get undressed with the team?" Valerie asks in a voice loud enough for the entire class to hear.

Silence for a few tortured seconds.

I feel my face heating up.

"I change in our locker room," I stammer, "the girls' locker room."

How lame! Valerie Holm accusing me of being a slut? Why didn't I say, "At least my clothes come off just for hockey practice—what's your excuse?"

No matter how badly I wished I'd come back at her, I don't dare. I'm hoping that if I let her use me as a verbal punching bag for a few rounds, she'll forget about my crack the other day and leave me alone.

I'm turning into such a coward.

It's too late to say anything now, anyway, and even Ms.

Freeman gives in and lets Valerie play the part of Caesar. Why do some people always seem to get their way?

Ms. Freeman turns from writing Valerie's name on the board, adjusts her glasses, and scans the rows of students. "Now, I'm looking for our Brutus."

I glance at Ms. Freeman at the exact moment she asks, "Jo, how about it?"

I'm tempted to say, "No thanks, I'll pass," but from the hopeful look on her face, I can see that's not an option. So I shrug and agree to the part, consoling myself with the thought of getting even with Valerie on stage.

If you're ever in doubt where you rank in the middle school social order, just take note of where you sit in the cafeteria. The Dereks and Valeries of our class occupy the rectangular tables on a platform along the back wall. From there, the athletes, cheerleaders, and rich kids look down on the rest of us, who sit at circular tables, ground level. Better known as the mosh pit.

Even though Ben and I play hockey and Taryn plays fast-pitch softball, there's more to being in the popular crowd than that. It also matters which side of town you live on, the style of clothes you wear, what country club your parents belong to, and the cars they drive.

"Never judge a book by its cover," Ms. Freeman always says, but she's wrong. In middle school, everyone does.

Lunch is at 11 A.M.—even though most of us call that breakfast on the weekends. Taryn's sitting at our table in the pit, unwrapping a tuna sandwich.

"What do you have?" she asks.

Taryn has had tuna for lunch every single day of school since first grade, even though she tells her mom at the beginning of every school year that she's sick of it.

But Mrs. Wu cheerfully insists, "Tuna's good for you. You don't like it? Make your own lunch."

Taryn would rather take her chances trading than wake up a minute earlier to pack a lunch.

I peek in my bag, relieved that Gramps didn't try anything creative today. "A bagel."

"What kind?" Taryn asks, leaning in for a closer look.

"Poppy seed with cream cheese."

"Nah, I hate poppy seeds. They get caught in my teeth." Taryn turns to Ben, who has a turkey sandwich he's not about to part with.

He refuses the trade but offers her some advice: "Tell your mom that you heard about mercury poisoning from eating too much tuna." He takes a bite of his sandwich. "Be sure to mention brain damage and lower SAT scores."

Taryn's not listening. She has her eye on a slice of pepperoni pizza two seats down and moves in for the sale before the kid snarfs it up.

"Tomorrow we find out who makes the team," Ben says to me.

We haven't spoken to each other since yesterday after practice, and I don't feel like talking about it now. What if one of us makes the team and the other one doesn't?

With a mouth full of bagel, I just nod. Taryn breaks the awkward silence with a victory dance. She's taken her chance on the lunch lottery and won.

"Yes!" she says, showing us the incredible trade for the soggy tuna—a chocolate cupcake with multicolored sprinkles.

Ben's not easily distracted. "Who would you pick for the team if you were coach?"

I shrug and say, "Don't know," which is a lie and Ben knows it. Since tryouts began, every night before I fall asleep, I compare my skills against every boy out there. I have my dream team, but I'm not talking.

"Okay, I get it," Ben says, as he stuffs the remainder of his lunch into his backpack. "I can take a hint." He stands up.

"Ben . . ." I want to tell him not to go, that I'm not angry with him, just angry with everything. Unfortunately, as he turns his back to leave, something flies across the cafeteria and hits me on the shoulder.

Ben doesn't see that that something is a meatball, part of the hot lunch menu that day. But he hears the howls of laughter from behind us on the platform where the cool kids sit. When Ben turns to see what the commotion is all about, Derek and his crowd are pointing and laughing at our table.

Ben's face reddens until it nearly matches the color of his hair. Public ridicule—just about the worst thing that can happen, and Ben probably thinks it's directed his way. Quickly, he walks out of the cafeteria without noticing the sauce dripping down my arm or the busted meatball on the floor.

"Hey! Somebody sneeze?" Derek shouts.

More laughter.

"Jerks!" Taryn says, as she hands me her napkin. She scoops

the meatball off the floor, turns, and fires it back at Derek's table like she's throwing someone out at the plate.

Unfortunately, another of Ms. Freeman's sayings, "The second one always gets caught," is true. The lunch monitors converge on our table and drag Taryn to the office, protesting and trailing sprinkles from her half-eaten cupcake.

Surrounded by the deafening roar of cafeteria noise and with ten minutes remaining in the lunch period, I consider two important questions: Will I be able to clean this sauce stain off my favorite sweatshirt? and Why is it so difficult to swallow food when you're eating all alone?

Four

"**S**wallow," my mom says softly to Franny, a patient she's taking care of at the nursing home. Franny opens her puckered mouth like a baby bird, and Mom dips the spoon into the liquefied dinner and offers it to her.

It reminds me of how she used to feed Michael in his high chair when he was a baby, except that there's no chance Franny will grab the spoon and say, "Me do it!"

Mom smiles when she notices me standing there, and says, "Hey kiddo, what's the occasion?"

I shrug. "I don't know. Just wanted to see you, I guess."

Eyebrows raised, she gives me a look that says if her hands weren't occupied, she'd check my forehead for a fever. She knows seeing her in her blue polyester uniform, stained from the work she performs feeding, cleaning, and toileting helpless old people all day, is not up there on my Top Ten list.

Usually Ben and I walk straight home after practice, passing the nursing home, rarely stopping for a visit. He wasn't waiting for me today after hockey practice, so I decided to stop in, even though this place can be depressing at times.

It's the old-people smell that hits you as soon as you enter the lobby, with its plastic seat cushions and white-haired bodies hunched in wheelchairs, many of them napping. A few are even tied into the chairs, cages on wheels, so they don't tumble out and hurt themselves.

In the commons room, they make craft projects, similar to the kind I once made in preschool, using a gallon of glue, Popsicle sticks, and yarn. Big band music from the 1940s plays in the background. I picture my classmates in nursing homes someday, listening to hip-hop and rap, slumped over our PlayStations and Xboxes, struggling to push the tiny buttons with arthritic fingers.

"How was practice today?" Mom asks as she sticks a straw into a can of nutritional drink and offers it to Franny.

"Okay," I tell her, and it was, except that Ben has become a master at the blind pass, refusing to look at me both on and off the ice. For faking out the defense, this is a good thing. For a friendship, well, it hurts to be invisible.

After dinner, Mom stays a little longer and helps Franny get ready for bed, combing out her silky white hair and tying it up in a ponytail. I feel a stab of jealousy watching them.

Franny talks about the faded photographs lined up on the dresser in her bedroom. I study an old wedding picture, the kind that looks like the color was painted on after the photo was taken. Pointing to a small gold frame, I ask, "Is that you, Franny, and your husband?"

"Yes, dear, that's my Frank, the love of my life for fifty-two wonderful years." She smiles and nods proudly. I can't believe that this fragile old woman and the glamorous young one in the photo are the same person.

I glance at the pictures of Franny's children, grandchildren, and one of Franny taken when she was my age. Something about this picture looks vaguely familiar to me, but who does it remind me of?

"You're beautiful, Franny," I tell her, and she reaches for my hands and gives them a gentle squeeze.

It's the end of Mom's shift and Franny hugs her good-bye. "'Night, 'night, sweetie pie," she says, kissing my mom on the cheek.

The lump in my throat is back again, and I stand there blinking back tears before they spill over.

As we leave Franny's room, Mom puts her hand on my shoulder. "What's the matter, Jo?"

"Nothing," I say as I wipe my eyes with the back of my sleeve. "I just never want to live in a nursing home, that's all."

"Hey," she smiles, giving my shoulder a quick squeeze, "let's worry about getting through middle school and high school first, okay?"

I nod in agreement.

Mom looks concerned but says, "I have to finish some paperwork for the next shift and then we'll head home."

I wait for her at the time clock where she slips her card in and punches out for the night. I want to tell her what happened at lunch today, but she looks so tired and has enough to think about.

Besides, what if she tells Dad? I can just see him storming into school, hunting Derek down. Who knows what he'd do? Pelt him with a dozen meatballs? Dump a bowl of spaghetti on his head? I smile, picturing the scene.

"So, practice went okay?" she asks for the second time, as if she senses I'm on an emotional roller coaster and not about to share the ride.

I'm just not ready to tell her about my run-ins with Derek, or the conversations with Lubic, Coach, Valerie, and Ben.

"It went fine," I say, and it's the truth. So, Ben and I aren't communicating much off the ice. Because we've skated together for seven years, though, we're still in synch *on* it, anticipating where the other will be in order to receive a pass or take a shot on goal.

Mom's car is at the mechanic's shop again, leaking antifreeze. So we turn left out of the parking lot and begin walking the couple of blocks home. It's so cold my eyeballs hurt, so I pull my scarf up over my mouth and nose.

Mom reaches over and brushes a few stray curls from my forehead as we walk home, side by side.

Normally, I don't like her fussing with my hair like I'm a baby, or one of her patients, but tonight I'd let her comb and braid my entire head.

As we walk along the sidewalk, I gaze into the windows of the houses on my street. Most are dark, except for the ones with the eerie flickering lights from the television.

I turn from the hypnotic scene when my mother says, "We didn't really have many sports opportunities when I was growing up."

She searches her coat pockets and continues, "I think I would have liked being part of a team." She pulls out a tissue and wipes her nose.

"I love being on a team. I just don't know if I've made a mistake trying out for this one."

"Why?" She looks surprised.

This is the first time she's heard me say anything negative about tryouts.

Standing in front of our home, I can see that the lights are off downstairs, but upstairs, Michael's bedroom light is on and the ceiling fan is spinning out of control.

We watch as a sock hits the fan blade and goes winging off into the air. Next, up flies a T-shirt. *Whump! Zing!* Followed by another sock.

Mom sighs, "What are we going to do with those two clowns?"

I follow her up the porch steps and wait as she searches for the keys in her bag. She says, "Jo, I'm glad you're trying out for hockey—*darn* it!" She digs deeper. "I can never find anything in here."

In spite of the cold, part of me wishes she'll never find the keys and we could stay outside a little while longer. I'd tell her what happened with Ben, and how angry I feel at Derek. Instead, I say, "Tomorrow I find out if I made it or not."

"In my eyes you already have—got 'em!" She holds up the keys and jingles them in front of me.

I notice a network of tiny lines around her mouth and dark shadows under her eyes. She looks tired under the dim porch light. She twists the house key into the lock and opens the door.

From behind, the light makes her flyaway hair look like an electric halo around her head. I recall the comments at school about her uniform and her job and I'm ashamed that I was embarrassed. I reach out for Mom, but she's already through the door.

I pause for a minute on the threshold and take a quick glance back across the street toward Ben's house. The light's on in his bedroom, but his shade is pulled.

"Tomorrow we'll know," I say out loud, "then everything will get back to normal."

"Jo!" Mom calls. "Shut the door. You're letting all the heat out."

I turn from the cold and step inside.

The next day, I'm up before my alarm rings, excited and nervous, with one thought running through my head—the list! Gramps is at the kitchen table drinking prune juice and eating canned corn with a spoon. I kiss the top of his head and note that at least he's dressed today, never mind that the plaid suit with the wide lapels looks like something he might have worn when he was in high school and it smells of mothballs.

Michael sits next to him in sweatpants and mismatched socks. Every last one he owns is strewn around his bedroom, thanks to the ceiling fan game. Finding a matching pair is pretty much out of the question this morning.

"Today's the 100th day of school party," he announces in between spoonfuls of Mighty Oats cereal. "I need to bring in 100 of something, in a bag, to count and share with my whole class . . . today."

"Michael, did you tell Mom?" I demand, glancing at the clock and watching my early start slip away.

"It's in the note," he says, pointing to his unopened backpack lying on the floor by the kitchen door.

Mom's upstairs sleeping and I don't want to wake her yet,

34

so I dump out the contents of Michael's cereal box on the kitchen table and grab a plastic sandwich bag from the drawer. "You've got to do your homework the night before, not at the last minute," I lecture him. "Start counting!"

Meanwhile, I grab an apple and a granola bar and shove them into my backpack for lunch since it doesn't look like Gramps made one for me today. I glance at Michael.

"Thirty-nine, forty-three . . . fifty," he says as he drops the tiny oat circles into the bag.

"Oh, no," I groan, and then I remember that, when I was in kindergarten, I barely knew my left hand from my right and tying my own shoelaces was out of the question.

I empty the plastic bag onto the table and say, "Gramps, please help Michael. He needs 100 of these in this bag for school today."

Then I race off to the bathroom to try to tame my wild hair and brush my teeth. "I don't want to be late," I whimper out loud. I've got to see if Ben and I made the team.

Back in the kitchen, Gramps is singing and counting, "Ninety-nine bottles of beer on the wall, ninety-nine bottles of beer . . ." as he empties fistfuls of cereal into the bag that Michael holds open for him.

What was I thinking? Last week Gramps had forgotten that he lives with us now and told the driver of the seniors' van to drop him off at his old house. He sat on the front porch until the new owners called Mom to come and take him home.

I run back into the bathroom and open the medicine cabinet and grab a plastic bag that says *100 Cotton Balls—100% Pure.* Entering the kitchen, I wave it above my head like a trophy. *"Ta-daaa!"* I say. "Hey guys, look what I found."

Michael and Gramps stop and stare as I stuff the cotton balls into Michael's backpack, saying, "One hundred cotton balls, Michael, you're all set."

Michael's not impressed. "I don't want dumb cotton balls. I want Mighty Oats and bottles-a-beer," he demands.

"Beer's out. You're underage, buddy, and Mighty Oats aren't good," I plead with him. "Look, they get crushed in your backpack and then you won't have one hundred." Frustrated, I smash a bunch of them with my fist and send the rest scattering across the table. "See?"

Wide-eyed, Michael nods, reluctantly agreeing to the cotton balls. "But they're Peter Cottontails," he insists.

"Fine. Whatever!" I glance at the clock and make quick *kiss-kiss* sounds above their heads, grab my backpack and hockey gear, and race out the door, struggling into my coat as I jog across the street.

I ring Ben's doorbell twice and stand there, stomping my feet on the porch, to keep them warm.

No answer.

"Darn it!" I say out loud. "I hope I didn't miss him." I jab my finger at the doorbell again and begin counting to one hundred in my head, willing Ben to appear. I'm on twenty-two when the door suddenly opens.

Mr. McCloud stands there in a dark business suit, looping a striped tie around his neck. "He's left already," he says.

"Oh, thanks. Sorry to bother you." I pick up my stuff and head down the steps, when he calls after me.

"You know something, I wish you pushy girls would just play your own sports and leave the boys alone." He tugs the knot up to the base of his neck and continues, "You don't see boys or grown men trying to barge their way into female sports, do you?"

I stand there on the bottom step, speechless, but he's not waiting for an answer.

"Like those hotshot women golfers, or those girls playing college football. Think they can play with the big boys. Huh?"

His neck and face turn a deep purple-red, as if his tie's choking him. "They learned their lesson and you will, too."

Without saying a word, I turn to go, but he's not through yet. Stepping outside onto the porch in his socks, he says, "Just leave Ben alone. You're not going to win this. You hear me?"

I don't look back, or even answer, yet like dealing with a rabid dog, I'd feel a lot safer if I could back out of this situation, keeping a close eye on him the entire time. He sounds like a biter.

The door slams and my friend the lump returns, settling in my throat, growing bigger with every swallow. As I walk along the sidewalk toward school, avoiding the uneven pavement that threatens to face-plant me into the concrete, I think I understand a little better why Ben's avoiding me. I can only imagine the topic of dinnertime conversation at the McCloud home.

But Ben's dad's got it wrong. It's not about winning or losing, at least the hockey part. It's about making the team, being a part of something that I'm good at and love. And it's about friendship, too, Ben's and mine. So he thinks I can't win, but I'm no quitter—and I'd do almost anything not to lose Ben.

Five

I arrive at school sweaty and trembling, determined to forget about Mr. McCloud. I hurry to the boys' locker room to see if I made the team. A small crowd has already gathered in front of a white sheet of paper taped to the door.

Trying to peer around people's heads, I see Derek's name at the top of the list—no surprise. The typed names aren't in alphabetical order. Quickly my eyes skip down the list reading the names: Sean Magaletta, Ryan Katz, and Ben McCloud—*"Yes!"* I say out loud.

A few heads turn. A couple of boys smirk at me and try to block my view.

I should be elated when I read the second-to-last name on the list—Joanna Giordano—but I'm not, because right next to it, someone has scrawled in blue ink the word "Dyke."

I feel a sick twisting in my gut and the heat rises to my face. Great—slut, dyke, what's next?

I try to rip the paper down, but someone pushes my arm away, saying, "Cut it out! People want to see who made the team."

I hear laughter and feel jostling from behind as more people crowd the door to inspect the list. I search in my backpack for some Wite-Out or a pen to scribble out the word, and someone bumps into me.

"Whoa! Sorry." Derek steadies himself. "Clumsy me. Hey, congratulations, teammate!" he says, holding out his hand for a shake.

I don't want to shake his hand. I'd rather spit in it and tell him that the next time he writes something next to my name, or throws a meatball, he better protect his own balls.

Swallowing hard, I push it all back down, because really, what proof do I have that it was Derek? Instead, I mutter, "Thanks."

I'm such a chicken! Tomorrow morning I'll wake up and find that I cluck and I've sprouted tail feathers out my butt.

"Hey, what's this?" Derek says, pointing to the word next to my name. He turns to his friends. "You guys know anyone named Dyke who tried out?"

Everyone laughs, except the boys who didn't make the team. They're too busy glaring at me and complaining bitterly to each other.

"Get out of my way," I say, pushing past Derek. Forget about whiting it out. Whoever hasn't seen it will certainly hear about it by the time first period ends.

Ben and I both made the team. That's the important thing. I just always pictured feeling a lot happier at this moment.

"Hey, Jo," Taryn calls after me as I weave my way through the crowded halls to my locker. "You made the team, girl. I made four bucks!" she says, giving me a high five.

"Yeah, great," I mutter.

"What's the matter?" she asks. "You upset about that 'dyke' thing next to your name?"

I nod.

"Ah, don't worry. I just scribbled it out. Now it says, 'Joanna Giordano, scribble-scribble.'" She smiles and crosses her arms. "Oh, and next to Derek's name? It says, 'wears girls' underwear.'"

I laugh, "You didn't!"

"No, but I wanted to. But I'm on probation for abuse of a meatball and attempting to incite a food fight in the cafeteria. Lubic didn't buy the self-defense plea."

"Thanks, Taryn. Thanks for everything." I turn the combination and ask, "Have you seen Ben?"

She smiles. "Yep"—hitching her thumbs in her jean pockets—"now that he's made the team, he's hangin' with the big boys at Monkey Island."

Monkey Island is the carpeted area in the middle of the main hallway of the school. The popular kids hang out on the maze of benches and quirky sculptures found there, while everyone else stands around paying homage to the alphas in the middle.

I know it's the wrong thing to do, even as I head there to look for Ben. I'll be late for class and I don't really know exactly how to tell him what I'm feeling. Somehow, "Congratulations, we made it! Let's be friends again" sounds way too chirpy after all we've been through.

But I figure the right words will come to me when I see him, and I'll just have to risk being late for study hall. Besides, Ms. Duzinski wouldn't care if everyone cut class—less hassle for her.

I spot Ben immediately, about twenty yards away, with his back toward me, leaning against a metal column talking to someone. As I get closer, I feel my heart racing and my hands sweating.

"Hey, McCloud!" I call out, and Ben turns toward my voice, but the minute the words are out of my mouth, I regret it.

"Hey, Jo," Ben says, giving me a smile.

Only, I'm not so sure if it's for me, or left over from the conversation he's having with Valerie Holm, who's dressed in jeans slung so low her silver navel stud sparkles and catches the light.

Where's the school dress code when you need one?

"Hi Jo-anna," Valerie says all fake and friendly as she leans across Ben and gives me a little wave like we're best buds.

I toss her a who-are-you-kidding look and a quick hello.

What could Ben and Valerie be talking about? She's probably said a total of two words to him in the last seven years of school, and now, all of a sudden, because he's made the hockey team, she's all over him.

I'm going to be sick.

But first I better come up with something other than breakfast, because my best friend and worst enemy are standing there waiting for me to say something—anything—and yet I'm frozen solid, speechless! Don't want to bring up hockey. Can't say any of the things I wanted to tell Ben.

Valerie, sensing my confusion, takes control. "I was just telling Ben about the Valentine's Day dance coming up," she says, placing her hand on his arm and flashing him a bleached smile.

Fully recovered now and thinking quick on my feet like an athlete should, I fire right back at her with a blistering, "Oh?"

"The cheerleaders are in charge of selling tickets and designing the decorations for the dance." She glances at Ben again—more smiles.

He smiles back.

Traitor!

I stink at this game. I blurt out much too loudly, "Ben!" and with what appears to be a supreme effort on his part, he tears himself away from Valerie's gravitational pull and turns his attention to me.

"Um . . ." Here's my chance, and the best I come up with is, "Say hi to your dad for me."

Exit Joanna, stage left, but not before I catch Valerie giving Ben a look that says she thinks I've taken one too many hits against the boards.

Weaving my way out of Monkey Island, avoiding backpacks, books, and outstretched legs in my path, I'm furious about Valerie, Ben, and that stupid Valentine's Day dance.

Thanks to Grandma Giordano, a big fan of martyrdom and suffering, who thought the *Book of Saints* is excellent bedtime reading for children, I recall that St. Valentine was a priest who got his head chopped off for defying the emperor and marrying young couples. So what's to celebrate about that?

And then it hits me.

Are Valerie and Ben going to the dance together?

I'm so upset at the idea that I don't pay attention to where I'm walking, and then, quite abruptly, I'm not. Tripping and falling over something in my path, I land in a pile of books and coats strewn all over the carpeted floor. Embarrassed, I quickly gather my things together, and that's when I hear his laugh and see the long legs stretched out near me.

"Clumsy today yourself, Jo," Derek says.

I look around to see if anyone saw what happened, but Ben is still basking in Valerie's attention. Even the young science teacher, who's supposed to be patrolling this area, is distracted on his watch by a gaggle of girls who get their kicks by flirting with cute teachers.

It's my call.

Maybe I really did trip over something other than Derek's legs thrown accidentally-on-purpose in my way. And maybe he wasn't the one who wrote "dyke" next to my name. There're plenty of other angry boys, some even cut from the team, who could have written it.

I sigh, grabbing my backpack and standing up. Maybe I should just put three years of self-defense training to use and knock Derek's nuts up around his earlobes.

Once again, I'm indecisive, and Derek's off and running free with his pack. Why do I always hesitate off the ice, when on it, I know without a doubt when I need to stand up for myself?

I curse him and vow to skate circles around him this afternoon at practice. If only I could wear my protective gear during the school day. "Zero tolerance for violence," Principal Lubic likes to proclaim in front of teachers, parents, and school board members, but in reality it's more like, "See no evil. Hear no evil. Speak no evil, and renew my contract!"

"Congratulations. You've made the team," Coach Granato says as soon as everyone whose name is on the list has gathered on the ice for the first official practice. "Now the hard work begins."

He's not kidding. We drill and scrimmage until I can barely lift my arms above my waist and my legs tremble and shake with every push off the ice.

"Smart pass, Giordano!" Coach calls to me. He slaps the back of my helmet as I skate past him, and suddenly I feel as if I could go another hour.

By the end of practice, though, I'm forced to acknowledge the unpleasant fact that, although I pass the puck to everyone on the ice, including Derek, unless I scrap for it and come up with it on my own, no one—not even Ben—passes to me. I'm the ghost girl on ice.

Coach must have noticed this, too, because at the end of practice, he gives a speech about how there's no "I" in the word "team."

"We're the Rams," he says, referring to our team mascot. "And Rams philosophy on and off the ice is: *Right Attitude Means Success!*"

Then everybody puts their hands in the middle and we do a lot of yelling and chanting, "Rams, Rams, Rams!"

I join in, but I still feel like I'm on the outside, wanting to believe that Coach's pep talk will unite us and solve everything, but knowing that it's going to take a lot more than a spelling lesson and a few chants to gain acceptance.

As we skate off the ice, I bump into Ben and say, "Good practice."

Everyone is relaxed and talking around us, unsnapping their sweaty helmets, thankful and excited to be on the team, but suddenly I'm aware that they're quiet. Are they listening for Ben's response to my comment?

"Yeah, thanks," Ben says and quickly turns away to ask Derek a question about an offensive play we'd been practicing.

That's it? Conversation's over before it has even begun.

Later, when I come out of the locker room, Ben isn't waiting for me in his usual spot to walk home. Instead, I catch a glimpse of his auburn hair up ahead with Derek and a group of his friends. They laugh and shove each other as they push open the doors and step out into the purple twilight of the setting winter sun.

I just stand there watching, willing Ben to look back and call my name, but he never even turns around.

Instead, Ms. Freeman comes down the hallway and says, "That you, Jo? I didn't recognize you with all that equipment. Going camping?"

"No, just finished practice," I say, as I transfer my hockey bag from one aching shoulder to the other and hoist my backpack off the floor.

"Hmm, heavy load," she says, although she's carrying two large canvas bags overflowing with papers and books. "We need those suitcases on wheels. The kind people zip around the airports with," she says with a chuckle, "or maybe a small golf cart that beeps when we go in reverse."

She's trying to be nice, but I can see her studying my face

45

and I know I'm probably rating negative numbers on the happiness scale.

"Will you walk with me to my car, Jo?"

I nod and follow her outside into the teacher's parking lot. Her car is a lime green Volkswagen Beetle with a pink poinsettia sticking out of a bud vase on the dashboard. Exactly what I'd picture her driving. I bet the silver Lincoln in the next space over is Lubic's.

"How's the team look?" Ms. Freeman asks as she pops open the trunk and loads her bags into the car.

"Good," I say. I bite down on my chapped lips in order to keep from blurting out my disappointment.

"Hmm, I see." Ms. Freeman nods sympathetically and then she launches into a speech about women disguising themselves as men and fighting during the Civil War and how Elizabeth Cady Stanton and Susan B. Anthony struggled for over forty years to get women the right to vote.

Hello? I want to interrupt and tell her, "It's not political. I just want to play hockey!"

She recommends some biographies for me to read: Eleanor Roosevelt, Rosa Parks, and Rachel Carson.

I don't think reading a bunch of books is going to save my friendship with Ben or make Derek respect me, Valerie accept me, or Lubic and Mr. McCloud think I'm anything but a pushy troublemaker. Yet Ms. Freeman looks so eager to help that I hear myself promising that I'll check them out. I guess for an English teacher there's no problem that a good book can't solve.

"I'd offer you a ride home, but it's against the rules," she says, glancing uneasily back at the school.

"It's okay," I tell her. "Do they have the parking lot under surveillance, too?"

"You bet," she laughs, "especially the teacher's parking lot."

"'Bye, Ms. Freeman, and thanks." I take off at a jog, hoping to catch up with Ben before he reaches home.

As I turn the corner onto our block, I see him three houses ahead, on his front porch. I drop my stuff and hurry across the street. "Hey, Ben!"

"Hey." He turns, acknowledging me with a slight lifting of his chin while he fumbles with the lock on his front door, balancing his hockey bag and backpack in his arms.

I stand there with my hands thrust deep into my pockets at the bottom of the steps, looking up at him, trying to think of something to say to make him stay outside and talk like we used to.

"Do you think we'll beat the Wildcats next week?" I ask, hoping it doesn't sound as desperate as I feel.

He shrugs. "Yeah, we could pull an upset."

"Yeah, an upset . . ." I agree with him. He watches me chipping away at some ice on the steps with the heel of my boot. Is he thinking that he'd rather be talking to Valerie about the dance than standing outside in the cold talking hockey?

As long as I've known Ben, we've never struggled to make conversation. Why is this so awkward? Has his father totally turned him against me? Or was it something that Derek or Valerie said to him?

We hear the crunching noise of tires running over ice. Mr. McCloud steers his car into the driveway, gives a stern look, and then drives behind the house to park in the detached garage.

"Gotta go. I have a ton of homework." Ben hesitates for just a moment and then says, "See ya, Jo" and quietly closes the door.

"Bye, Ben."

Standing there in front of his house, I feel like Mrs. Stritch's goose statue. Would anyone bother to dress me for the holidays? Valentine's Day's coming soon. I think a sweater with a giant broken heart sewn on it would just about say it all.

Snow begins to fall and I feel the cold flakes brush against my face before they melt away. A steady stream of headlights passes before me, people returning home from work.

"Books are your friends," Ms. Freeman always says. This used to sound so corny to me. I remember seeing an Eleanor Roosevelt biography on the shelf in Gramps's room. I think it belonged to Grandma Giordano. I decide to look for the book after dinner, maybe even read a few pages.

Sure, books are our friends, and with the way things have been going lately, I can use all the friends I can get. I wonder what *The Great Gilly Hopkins* or *Harriet the Spy* would do if they were in my shoes.

Six

When I open my locker the next morning, I just stand there for a minute, stunned, not comprehending what I'm seeing. I check the outside number to make sure it's mine—156. Yep, the same one I was assigned on the first day of seventh grade.

The outside's the same, but the inside looks totally different. It's covered in deep red tissue paper, with a small oval mirror attached to the door, along with a sprig of some kind of plant—bamboo? All my books are neatly stacked and recovered in jewel-toned paper. Sitting on top of them is a green velvet bag.

I pick it up and smell it—lavender?

Hanging from my coat hook is a tiny metal wind chime with three carved doves on top.

"Taryn!" I say her name out loud.

She peeks her head out from around the corner. "You called?"

She's been watching my reaction the whole time.

"What did you do to my locker?" I demand, but I'm laughing because when I touch the bird chimes they make the sweetest musical sound.

"It's a feng shui makeover, Jo, and it'll change your life!" She runs her finger across the chimes and they sing out again.

"I've had enough change. I want things to go back to the way they were," I tell her, but secretly I'm pleased. Maybe bright colors and chimes are the answers to all my problems.

Taryn pouts. "You don't like it?"

"No, I love it. Thanks, Taryn, but I can't promise you that I'll be able to keep my books and everything as neat and organized as you have them right now."

Taryn checks out her hair and adjusts her quirky earrings in the mirror and smiles. "See?" She points to her reflection. "Things are lookin' good already!"

I laugh and grab a few books, careful not to disturb anything, and then slam the door closed, but some red tissue paper gets caught. I try to push it back in through the crack. No luck. I retry the combination and give it my usual shoulder check. It refuses to open.

"It's jammed!" I cry.

Taryn shrugs. "Give it a chance."

I rip the excess red paper off and shove it in my pocket. "I guess I'll carry my good luck with me," I tell her as I hurry down the hall, late for math.

Pre-algebra is a joke. Mr. Plotkin's the worst teacher in the school. Not because he doesn't know math. The problem is he can't control the class, so nothing ever gets done. Besides, it's hard to respect a teacher who carries an eraser and chalk in a plastic bag tied to his belt buckle.

Every morning, Plotkin comes in and writes the class

work and homework on the board, but in the chaos between the bells, students walk by and change the assignments by adding a page number here, erasing problem numbers there. Plotkin begins every class by saying, "Now, who did that?"

You'd think he'd wise up and use an overhead projector or something. Nope, Plotkin's solution is the bag-o-chalk, which he dutifully caddies around on his belt in an attempt to prohibit student editing. But schools spawn chalk, and a quick swipe of the hand works just as well as an eraser.

Even the math geeks laugh at him from their front-row seats. It's a sure sign that a teacher should retire when even the brainiacs revolt. Sometimes, I wish Plotkin would stand up for himself, throw someone out, give a few detentions—anything.

After Pre-al is English, and I fear Ms. Freemen will be waiting at her door with a bag full of women's biographies and a year's worth of *Ms.* magazine back issues. It's not that I don't appreciate her concern. It's just that she looks at my playing hockey as some kind of girl-power statement, when all I want to do is get in the game, skate fast and strong, maybe score a few goals, and not be treated like I'm a freak on ice.

Sure enough, Ms. Freeman is waiting at the door—but empty-handed, greeting all her students as they arrive for class. She gives me smiles. No study guide required.

I take my seat and overhear Valerie telling Heather and Courtney that everyone should call Ms. Freeman "Ms. Free-woman" instead. I have to admit Valerie's got a point. It fits.

We break into small groups to rehearse our lines for *Julius*

Caesar. Ben and Taryn have smaller roles and go off in a group of their own, while I'm stuck with Valerie, who announces, "I think we should definitely wear white togas for the performance."

"Who uses plain white sheets anymore?" Courtney asks as she hunches over her pocketbook mirror, applying eye shadow.

"I bet Jo can get some from her mother at the nursing home. She changes the beds there, doesn't she, Jo?" Valerie asks.

I squeeze Taryn's lucky red paper in my pocket. Its positive chi, or whatever Taryn calls it, is not powerful enough to ward off negative Valerie vibes. Maybe I'd have better luck wearing the wind chimes around my neck.

"Sometimes my mother changes sheets," I answer Valerie, "but only when they're soiled with vomit, urine, blood, or crap. You wouldn't want those, would you?"

Valerie stares at me like I'm out of my mind.

And I am.

I bet her mother's never even changed a diaper. I've seen Mrs. Holm zipping around town with one manicured hand on the steering wheel of her Mercedes SUV and the other holding a cell phone to her diamond-studded ear. President of the PTA, Valerie's mom struts around the school in high heels, perpetually tan, dressed in Valerie's clothes and insisting that everyone, including students, call her Margo.

"Nooo, thank you," Valerie says, determined to have the last word on the subject. "But, ask her if we can borrow some *clean* white sheets, without having to take them off your own beds, of course."

What I'd love to ask Valerie is, "What did I ever do to you? And how the hell do you know what color sheets they have at the nursing home?"

After English and before Discovering Technology, I try my locker again to see if it'll open.

Stuck!

How does Taryn's mom make a living off this feng shui stuff? Then again, maybe my color's not red.

On my way to class, I turn in my locker number at the office so a janitor can use the Jaws of Life and pry the sucker open and I can finally get at my books.

Mr. Spitzer gives me a zero in Discover Tech for being unprepared, even though I try to tell him my locker's jammed. Apparently, he's heard that one before. Why do so many teachers think *guilty until proven innocent* instead of the other way around?

Four of my teachers joke that they're the "century team" because, among them, they have over a hundred years of teaching experience. I guess if I'd spent that many years in a middle school classroom, even a simple "Good morning" from a student would begin to sound suspicious to me.

I take my seat next to Brendan Mitchell, a quiet boy with a voice so high that everyone calls him Mouse. "You can share with me." He places his textbook between our computers.

"Thanks." I glance around the room and see Derek and a couple of his friends joking around in the back row.

"Good luck in the game tomorrow night," Brendan squeaks. "I hope you score a goal."

He's talking and typing at incredible speeds and I bet he hasn't made one mistake, and here I am on the second line and have had to hit *delete* three times already in order to correct errors.

"Thanks," I say, but I'm not really focused on Brendan or my work. I'm thinking about the game, wondering how I can do well when no one passes to me. I worry about my dad's behavior, too. He's been so hyped-up ever since he heard that I made the team, that I'm afraid he's due for one of his spectacular public displays of poor sportsmanship.

"Time's up!" Spitzer calls and we hit the *print* buttons and turn in our work.

For the remainder of class, we're free to play computer games, while Spitzer surfs e-Bay for *Star Trek* memorabilia. The boys usually choose Battle Star Universe or Age of Warriors, while the girls create their own Sim-Families, or just hang out in small groups styling each other's hair, painting nails, or applying makeup. Spitzer doesn't care, just as long as they're quiet.

I'd rather battle it out with the boys' computer games. At least there, the rules of engagement are clear-cut and have definite goals. Besides, I grew up playing war games with my older brother. I mean, how do you "win" Sim-Family? "Na, na—my family's richer, smarter, prettier than yours!"

No thanks, too close to real life for me.

The boys are arguing about partners for Battle Star Universe, while Spitzer looks up from his screen and warns, "Keep it down."

I want to join them but am not sure if I have the energy to push it, especially since Derek's obviously in charge.

Brendan hovers on the fringe of the boys' noisy group,

hoping they'll notice him and put him on a team. He probably has the only A-plus in class and the fastest fingers in the school, yet they'll completely ignore him because in their eyes he's just Mouse.

I sigh and begin typing a letter to my brother at college. I have more in common with Brendan Mitchell, and I don't even have the courage to ask him to play Battle Star Universe with me because of how everybody else looks down on him.

So, I wonder, who's the real mouse?

Ben's a no-show at lunch again.

Taryn says, "McCloud's cute, but he's so skinny he can't afford to miss a meal"; then she takes off on her daily tuna mission.

I miss Ben. My stomach growls in agreement.

In a few minutes, Taryn returns to the table with a banana-strawberry yogurt—the tuna's history. "Here's to making the Honor Roll this quarter," she says, raising the cup in the air.

Immediately, a lunch monitor zeroes in on our table, giving Taryn the evil eye.

"I'm a marked woman," Taryn complains. "I bet I can't even scratch my head without one of these blue-haired mamas freaking out and writing me up."

Then she deliberately scratches her head to test her theory, giving the monitors an exaggerated smile.

I want to tell Taryn to cut it out. If she's kicked out again, where will that leave me? I say nothing to Taryn, though, and open my lunch bag and take out another bagel, only this time it looks like cinnamon raisin with peanut butter and broccoli stuck in between. "Oh, no," I say, opening the sandwich and picking out the broccoli pieces one by one. Gramps definitely crossed the line with this combo.

"Eew," Taryn says, leaning over and wrinkling her nose, "that's a tough trade."

"I'm not that hungry, anyway." I spend the rest of the lunch period scanning the tables, wondering where Ben's at. He's not in the pit or sitting with his newfound friends, Derek and company. "Where do you think Ben eats?" I ask Taryn.

"Maybe he went to the library to do some research, or he's making up work in science lab," she suggests.

Who am I kidding? He's avoiding me. How do you try to make up with someone when he pulls a Houdini and disappears from your life?

I'll just have to be patient and wait for a chance to talk to him. At least I know there's one place we're bound to bump into each other—on the ice.

"Get your stick in there, Giordano! You've got to fight for possession harder than that!" Coach Granato shouts from the middle of the rink.

I'm going against Derek in the drill, but this time, he gives it his all and doesn't let up on me for a minute. We battle for the puck and I lose my balance and crash to the ice. This time, there's no blood and dizziness. I get back up on my skates and continue playing. I'm so happy I feel as if I'm flying.

"Pay attention! Look up! Pass, pass, pass!" Coach barks

orders at us in preparation for tomorrow night's game against the Wildcats.

We skate hard, anticipating the match, each of us dreaming of defeating a team that's supposed to skate circles around us.

I like being the underdog. Let them underestimate us. They're on top, living off last season's glory, which only makes me want to fight harder to bring them down.

At the end of practice, Coach gathers us all together. "No one expects you to win," he says, looking each one of us in the eye, "but that's not what *I* expect. If you skate your hearts out tomorrow night, fight for every possession, and come together as a team, I guarantee you'll walk off the ice winners!"

We solemnly listen to every word he says like it's a prayer. Not even Derek dares to make a wisecrack. I don't want to let Coach down. After all, he's taken a chance on me, and at this moment, I feel strong and hopeful that everything he says will come true.

I'm disappointed, but not surprised, when I come out of the girls' locker room after such a great practice and find the hallway empty. I guess I thought that warm fuzzy team feeling we had going on out there would carry over into my relationship with Ben. But he's nowhere in sight.

I glance up and down the hallway, half hoping that Ms. Freeman will appear, but it's later than usual and she's probably left school already.

Suddenly, I feel sad listening to my footsteps echo off the metal lockers as I walk down the hall. It's the loneliest sound I've ever heard.

When I open the exit doors, a blast of icy February wind tries to force me back inside. I struggle forward, tucking my chin under my scarf and bracing myself for the walk home.

The minute I open my front door, I know something's wrong. No funny smells or laughter coming from the kitchen, and Michael is crouched in the corner of the living room, still dressed in his coat, gloves, and boots from school.

"Jo!" he cries when he sees me, and charges forward, grabbing my hands and pulling me to the stairs. "Gramps is mad at the guy in the mirror. He's yelling at him. I'm scared."

I can see from Michael's red-streaked face that he's been crying. I drop my hockey gear and books on the floor and dash up the steps two at a time. The door's open and the light's on in the bathroom. Gramps is standing in his pajamas in front of the mirror over the sink.

"Bastard, get out of here!" he shouts at his own reflection, jabbing his finger at the glass. "You get away. You . . . stole it!"

I stand in the doorway shocked, because in all my life, I've never seen Gramps angry. Even when Jim and I smashed a hockey puck through the garage window at his old house, he never raised his voice. "Don't worry, it was an accident," he told us.

Who is this stranger cursing and yelling at a mirror?

Gently, I touch his arm, but he roughly pushes it away, becoming even more agitated. My heart's pounding and I'm frightened now, too.

"How long has he been like this?" I ask Michael, who

stands farther back in the hallway, refusing to come any closer.

"When I got home from school," and then very quietly he adds, "Gramps messed his room."

"I'll be right back, Gramps." But he doesn't even look at me, just continues to mumble and shout at the mirror.

I cross the hallway to Jim's old bedroom. Gramps's clothes, which were in the dresser drawers, are scattered everywhere. The metal reading lamp is lying twisted and broken on the floor, shards of glass stick out of the carpet. The hockey posters that once covered Jim's walls look as if a tiger has clawed them; most are ripped and torn on the floor.

A fishy, foul odor, like the kind you smell in the bus-stop shelter, is coming from a large stain on the carpet. My first thought is that somebody broke into our home. Somebody robbed us. But then I realize that Michael's right—Gramps did this—and my teeth start to chatter, even though I'm standing here in my winter coat, sweating.

A loud crash comes from the bathroom. I run back to Gramps, passing Michael in the narrow hallway. I tell him, "Call Mom!"

Michael stands there crying. "Please don't do that, Gramps," he sobs as Gramps opens and slams the medicine cabinet mirror, knocking its contents onto the floor.

"Come out! Out!" Gramps howls as he flails away, sending aspirin, toothpaste, creams, and a bottle of Pepto-Bismol crashing to the tile below. Suddenly, he slips on the mess and falls.

"Michael," I yell, giving him a push toward the stairs, "call

Mom at work, now!" He disappears around the corner. I hear the receding sounds of his boots clomping down the steps.

With one arm around Gramps and the other clinging to the side of the bathtub like it's a lifeboat, I hold him as he groans. Somewhat calmer after his fall, he desperately searches my face. But he doesn't even seem to recognize me, let alone find any comfort there.

It seems like Michael's gone a lifetime before I hear the sirens and see the pulsing red-blue lights reflecting off the plastic shower curtain. "They're here, Gramps," I whisper to him. "Help's here."

Exhausted and shivering, he clutches my hand and curls toward me on the cold tile floor, among the broken bottles, pills, and sticky pink puddles of medicine. Under his breath, he mumbles a constant stream of gibberish, words with no connection to each other or the chaos around us.

I kneel next to him, stroking his matted white hair, and say over and over again, "It's okay, Gramps. Everything's going to be okay."

I count the number of black and white tiles on the floor, desperate to pass the few remaining seconds until Mom comes and takes charge.

The minute she bursts into the room with the paramedics and police officer crowding right behind her, I take one look at her terrified expression and I know that I've been telling Gramps and myself a lie—everything's not going to be okay.

I hold Gramps tight as the paramedic rips his favorite pin-striped pajamas and sticks a needle into his leg.

"I'm so sorry, Jo, so sorry," Mom sobs, reaching for me.

She doesn't address Gramps or even say his name. I think she knows he's been slipping away from us for months now. I think we both knew.

The paramedic finishes taking Gramps's vital signs and signals to me that he's ready to transfer him to the gurney and then outside to the waiting ambulance.

But I'm not ready to let go. I cradle his head in my arms and hope that Gramps doesn't mind that my tears are falling all over his beautiful, sad face.

Seven

*F*unny how sometimes the thing you've wanted so badly in your life, when you finally have it, doesn't seem as important, or as wonderful, as you once imagined it would be.

Here I am tonight, starting the first game of the season, waiting for the face-off on center ice, and all I can do is look up into the stands and think about what's missing—Gramps. He's in the hospital, while they run some tests and find out what's wrong.

I try to block it out of my mind and focus on the game that's about to begin, but I'm so nervous and worried that I wish I had one last chance to use the bathroom before the ref blows the whistle. I look down the line and see Ben over on the left wing and Derek in the middle, both of them tense and waiting.

And then there's my dad.

He's sitting up in the stands wearing a red sweater, even though our school colors are purple and gold. He insists on wearing it, though, because it was his father's sweater and he believes it brings good luck. It's not like he's the sentimental type. It's just that he'd do anything to bring home a win.

Mom's still at the hospital with Gramps. Michael is sitting

on one side of Dad, while Taryn's on the other, probably complimenting him on the positive energy that the color red evokes.

Who knows, maybe in the heat of the game Taryn will be a calming influence: "Deep breaths, Mr. Giordano! Only kind words for the refs, please!"

She'd have better luck with pepper spray and a muzzle.

Coach is grinning like he knows a wonderful secret, something the rest of the town can't even begin to imagine—we can win this game! It doesn't matter that the team we're up against went undefeated last year, or that a moment ago, his own team was surprised and angry to learn that a girl is starting on the front line tonight for the Rams.

None of this means anything to Coach. The simple fact is that he believes we can win. The rest is up to us.

After his pregame talk, he pulls me aside and says, "Jo, I had my doubts at first, but tonight I wish I had six of you out there. You've got speed, skill, and moxie—and that's what'll win it for us!"

Then he raps me on the helmet with his hand and walks over to talk to Derek.

I say the word out loud, "moxie," liking the sound and feel of it on my lips. I'm not exactly sure what it means, but if Coach thinks it'll help, I'm glad I've got it.

The ref holds the whistle between his teeth and prepares to drop the puck, just as I catch a glimpse of my brother Jim entering the arena. My stomach does a 360. He wasn't supposed to be home again until spring break, and yet here he is for my first game!

I don't have much time to think about his arrival before

the whistle blows and the puck is slapped off a Wildcat stick and skids across the ice.

For the first six minutes of the game, the Wildcats dominate. Every time I go for the puck, I lose the battle and come up empty. They take ten shots on goal to our two, and when I glance up into the stands, I see that my dad's so worked up his face is two shades darker than his lucky sweater.

With just 2:14 left to go in the first period, Derek struggles to move the puck up the ice, looking for an open player. Adrenaline surges through my body. I break away from my defender and find myself open in the middle, hoping for the centering pass that I could one-time into the net.

The pass never comes.

Derek glances at me and then twists around, searching for the other wing, who's still back in our zone scrambling with another player.

I slap my stick against the ice, calling for the puck and shouting, "Derek—here!"

Coach, too, sees that I'm open, because I hear him yelling to Derek from the bench: "Jo—in the middle!"

From somewhere in the stands, it sounds like a wild animal is in pain, the cry is so loud, tortured—and familiar.

A second later, the opportunity's gone.

The Wildcats steal the puck from Derek and quickly move it up the ice to set up a goal. Ben skates back to try to help out on defense, but the Wildcats' blue jerseys swarm in front of our goalie. There's trash talking, shoving, pushing, and then a loud *crack*.

Shot on goal!

The puck's deflected in front of the net and a Wildcat player slaps it home.

Wildcats 1, Rams 0.

Out of the corner of my eye, I see Derek angrily bang his stick against the ice and curse.

I look up into the packed arena. Dad's on his feet shouting, his face has moved beyond red to a scary shade of purple. Jim is sitting beside him, pulling at his sleeve to try to get him to sit down.

Michael's hand reaches repeatedly from his mouth to a super-sized bag of popcorn, as he sits there patiently waiting for his favorite part of the game, when the Zamboni cleans the ice.

Taryn's given up on trying to soothe my father. She now sits on the other side of Jim, who gives me a thumbs-up.

I smile and wave at him and skate back to center ice for the drop, trying to push the thought of what Gramps is doing right now out of my mind.

Get the puck, Jo, I chant to myself over and over, because I know at this point in the game, down by a goal, I'd have to be the last person standing on the ice before any of my teammates passes it my way.

At the sound of the whistle, I skate off in a full tear toward the left side, anticipating Derek ignoring me once again on the right. Unfortunately, the Wildcats have picked up on his tendency to favor the left as well, and I find myself battling among three Wildcat players for the elusive puck.

Suddenly, it pops out of the mayhem and skitters away. I race after it and the next thing I know, I'm drilled hard from behind, crash to the ice, and slide into the boards with a sickening *thud*.

There's no whistle, and the ref doesn't call a penalty.

Struggling to get back on my feet, I hear a terrible howl fill the arena.

I don't need to look in his direction. Maybe it's the frustration from watching me trying to get a pass from my own teammates and failing. Maybe it's because he can't find a job, the separation, or the simple fact that we're losing.

Whatever the reason, I see a red sleeve wind up and throw something that arcs high into the air and seems to travel above our heads in slow motion until it lands with a crushing explosion of ice, plastic, and cola spraying all over and staining the ice a deep liquid brown.

In my head, there's a deafening silence.

I close my eyes, willing this ugly scene away. Now, it's me who's taking deep breaths, thankful that they come at all, one after the other, and when I open my eyes again, I see the black-and-white stripes of the ref's uniform skating by in a blur to the scorer's table, and then there's an announcement booming over the PA system. Some of it filters through, like the words "violation" and "prosecuted to the fullest extent of the law."

To make the point perfectly clear, a uniformed police officer escorts the man in the red sweater toward the exit doors. My brother Jim's alongside them, arguing, following him out.

I want to shout, "Jim, don't go!" but I'm frozen to the ice in shame.

Everyone knows it's my father, but I pretend that underneath my uniform, helmet, and pads, I'm protected and anonymous. "Go ahead, take him away. Lock him up and never let him near me again."

We're still down by a goal and I'm so furious at my dad that I feel sorry for any guy who crosses my path now. After the ice is cleaned of my father's carbonated bomb, Coach calls us over for a talk, the one where he points out that there's no "I" in "team."

I glance at Derek, pretty sure that this one is going right over his head again, based on his spelling aptitude and his huge ego.

I wind up sitting for most of the second period, trying to calm myself and forget about my father.

Ten minutes later, the Zamboni, a beautiful beast of a machine, comes roaring out of its cavern at the far corner of the arena. Pumped up on propane, its blades cut the surface clean and smooth over all traces of the struggle.

Before the first line skates back out for the final period, Coach grabs my arm and asks, "You okay, Joanna?"

I nod but refuse to look him in the eye. I'd break down if I saw even a trace of pity there.

"You were fouled," Coach says. "The ref missed the call. Your dad just didn't handle it right."

"Never does," I say. I step back onto the ice and skate hard to my position.

Derek catches my eye before the drop, spits, and mouths the words, "Where's your daddy?"

I shoot back, "Pass, you ass!"

He snorts and laughs out loud.

Great, I amuse him. Doesn't Derek, the hockey god, realize we're down by a goal? Doesn't he care if we win or lose?

The ref cups his hands over his mouth and blows two quick warming breaths into them. A second later, the whistle shrills and the puck is dropped in between Derek and a Wildcat player.

Their sticks crack together like a thunderclap.

Derek wins the face-off and barrels down the ice to the opponent's goal, displaying amazing stick skills as he sends it into the boards and collects his own rebound. He's double-teamed, but reverses direction and dumps it off to Ben, who has skated up along the outside and slaps it into the back of the net.

Our fans leap to their feet, cheering and stomping the aluminum bleachers as the deafening noise vibrates throughout the arena.

Tie game.

"Great shot, Ben!" I slap his glove and congratulate him as we return to center ice. For the first time in a long while, he flashes his old familiar grin.

Derek skates by, gloved hands holding his stick high above his head, celebrating as if he had just won the Olympic gold. "Like that pass, Jo-Jo?" he asks.

I smile and shake my head. I really wish I could hate him, but I can't. I'm saving all my fury for my father.

I glance up into the stands and see that Jim's back—good. Hopefully, Dad's safely behind bars. Now, if I can just get a stick on that puck and score a goal, we could beat this team and Jim wouldn't have wasted his time coming all this way to see me play. Also, it would prove to Lubic and everyone else that I belong out here, and best of all—my dad would feel horrible for getting thrown out and missing it.

Revenge is highly motivating.

The whistle blows and for the next eight minutes, we're scrambling all over the rink, ice spraying, sticks flying, desperately trying to put something together.

Shot! Deflected.

Shot! Wide.

Shot! Saved.

With two minutes left in the game, two Wildcat players sandwich Ben into the boards—*crash! Bang!*

Ben falls to the ice, grabbing his shoulder and twisting in pain.

I'd rather be the one hurt than see someone I care for suffering.

I skate over to him and try to help Ben up as he holds his right shoulder and Coach substitutes a player for his position.

One minute left. Tie game and both teams are on fire.

"Hey, Jo, got some *mojo* left in ya?" Derek asks as we line up for what may very well be the last drop in regulation play.

I nod. Sweat burns my eyes. I bite down on my mouth guard and grip my stick even tighter. We're too tired for overtime and too competitive to be satisfied with a tie.

Derek wins the draw. I feel as if I'm flying over the ice, so completely focused on that spinning puck that it catches me by surprise when I extend my stick and it's there at my feet.

I'm checked hard on my left side, but somehow manage

to battle my way through, retaining possession of that beautiful whirling black disk. It's a semi-breakaway, and quickly I skate into the Wildcat defensive zone and see the net less than twenty feet ahead of me.

With my peripheral vision, I notice Derek to my left, fighting his way through his defender and clear for an open shot on goal.

He raps his stick on the ice, calling for the puck. I hesitate for a second. This is *my* chance and I'm not giving it up! He's frozen me out since day one and now he expects me to pass to him!

The goalie comes out of the box, cutting my angle, leaving Derek alone in front of the net.

I make a decision and pull back with my stick and send the puck shooting across the ice, exactly where I meant to aim it—in front of my teammate's stick.

With a quick wrist shot, Derek one-times the puck into the Wildcats' net for the winning goal.

The buzzer sounds. Rams 2, Wildcats 1.

Derek skates in front of the net, pumping his stick in the air until our team piles on top of him, slapping his back and celebrating. "You're the man! Awesome goal!"

Our fans are on their feet again, clapping and cheering while they watch us celebrate the first victory of the season.

I'm thrilled that we won, but now that the game is over, I feel lost out here on the ice. I search for Ben and catch a glimpse of him with ice on his shoulder, his arm taped against his chest as he leaves the bench with the trainer.

I hope he's not badly hurt. I skate toward him, but Coach steps out onto the ice and gives me a big hug. "That a girl, Jo—you did it! Beautiful teamwork. Just beautiful!" he says.

The rest of the team gathers around, laughing, joking, reliving every important play and making plans for celebrating after the game. No one asks me to join them.

Coach shouts over the excited talk, "You kids really proved yourselves tonight and I'm proud of each and every one of you!"

I collect my stuff under the bench and make my way to the girls' locker room to change and meet up with my family. I'm almost to the locker room door, when I hear a voice from behind shouting, "Hey, wait up!"

Derek is standing there alone, a sweaty, grinning mess.

"You know, if I were you, I wouldn't have passed," he says, all out of breath. "I would have taken that shot for myself."

"Yeah, I know," I say, pulling off one of my gloves and pausing to look him in the eye, "but you would have missed."

"Ha!" he laughs, and rubs his hands through his hair. "Anyway, nice pass, Jo."

"Thanks, good game." I turn and enter the girls' locker room, catching a glimpse of myself as I walk in front of the mirrors.

I'm smiling.

Eight

Mom's working today, so Jim and I get up early to catch the Rapid Transit to the Greyhound bus terminal downtown. We stayed up talking about Dad, Gramps, and hockey until 2 this morning. Whenever I think about Jim having to go back to school, I feel as if someone has their hands wrapped around my neck and they're about to squeeze.

Before Jim went away to college, we'd fight sometimes, but there was no one I admired or wanted to impress more. I know it sounds pathetic, but somehow my life doesn't seem completely real without Jim here to share in it.

Dad? Well, that scene was all too real last night. Which is one of the reasons Jim chose to attend a college six hours away. They never got along. Instead of feeling proud of Jim's winning a scholarship, Dad saw it as competition. Whenever they'd argue, Dad would say, "You want to take it outside right now and race?"

As if crossing the finish line ahead of his teenage son would somehow settle the matter in his favor. Jim always refused. Just once, I wished he had taken Dad up on it and dusted him.

I remember one time sitting in the stands with Mom, watching Dad coach Jim's Little League game and seeing Dad give the signal to steal second base.

Jim didn't move.

Dad signals him again, and still Jim's glued to first base.

Dad calls a time-out and walks over to Jim, grabbing his uniform at the neck and shaking him around a little like a rag doll. "I'm the coach," he says. "You listen to me when I tell you to steal!"

Then he turns to the parents watching in the stands and says, "Don't worry, he's my son."

Or the time he grabbed Jim's face mask during a peewee football game and yanked him down to the ground like he was making an obstinate dog heel. No one ever tried to stop my father when he did these things. The only thing that slowed him down was when Mom asked him to leave.

Dad's basically had a choke chain on Jim his entire life. Now that Jim's escaped by going to college, Dad seems to be focusing his attention on me and the sports I play. I should warn Michael to stay away from athletics altogether. Take cooking classes. Join the marching band. Keep Dad off your back for life.

We arrive at the bus terminal and take a seat on long wooden benches with high backs and scrolled arms. They remind me of church pews, except you wouldn't find "Smit Dog loves LaQuita" carved into the benches at St. Anthony's. It's been so long since I've gone to Mass that I probably wouldn't remember what to do. Still, I'm tempted to sit here and pray that the bus never comes to take Jim away, or at least that it's running very late.

"You did great last night," Jim says for the fifth time. "You're fearless out there. I'm proud of you." He slings his arm over my shoulder and gives it a squeeze.

I study his profile. I had never really noticed how good-looking my brother is until Taryn said to me after the game, "He's so hot. His blue eyes, his dark curly hair. Oh, my God, when he smiles!"

I don't tell Jim that he's wrong about me being brave. Most of the time, I'm just trying to fit in and avoid getting hassled by the popular kids—like everyone else at school. But, like Eleanor Roosevelt says, sometimes you have to make a choice—either stand up or sit down for your beliefs.

A dirty bus pulls up outside the terminal, its wheels squealing as it comes to a stop, spewing a blast of foul-smelling smoke from its back end.

Jim gathers his canvas duffel bag in one arm and pulls me close with the other. "Thanks for waiting with me, Jo," he says into my hair. He takes a step back and studies my face. "You okay, Sis?"

I can only nod, because I'm crying like a big baby and I know Jim doesn't have the time right now for a drama queen. Reaching into his back pocket, he takes out his faded red bandana and wipes at my tears, then hands it to me.

The bus lets out another noxious blast and I burrow my head into his shoulder, trying to hold back my sobs, but only managing to make strangled snorting noises into his armpit.

"Hey, Miss Piggy?" He laughs and hugs me close for a second, then whispers, "You're a strong girl, Jo. Everything's going to be okay."

I lean my cheek against the cold window on the train ride back home and try to make out the words of the neon-colored graffiti spray-painted on the tunnel walls, railcars, and abandoned buildings. With Michael at a friend's and Gramps in the hospital, I decide to go to the nursing home and help Mom rather than return to an empty house.

When I arrive, I tell the receptionist, Charlotte, that I'm here to see Mom. She smiles and says, "Great game last night, honey!"

Besides school sporting events, there's not a lot to do on a Friday evening in our town. Many older adults whose children have long since graduated from school and moved away still attend football, basketball, and hockey games, just as they once did when their own children were competing. I guess it makes them feel like they're still a part of it all.

I find Mom organizing the lunch trays and nutritional supplements for the patients. Overcooked green beans, a little on the gray side, sit with applesauce, rice, and a mystery meat on each tray. No wonder no one wants to eat around here.

For dessert, there's green Jell-O cubes doing a little shimmy in a side bowl, capped with a jaunty squirt of whipped cream. I hope it's real cream and not the chemical-in-a-can kind.

Mom glances up from the trays. "Jim make his bus all right?"

"Yes." I touch the bandana he gave me, which I've tied around my neck. If Mom recognizes it or notices my red, swollen eyes, she doesn't say anything.

Instead she hands me a tray. "Take this over to Franny, please."

I survey the tables, which are surrounded by walkers, canes, and wheelchairs, with their owners looking like shrunken kindergarteners patiently awaiting their food, yet having little say as to what time they eat or what's being served. Are they sitting with friends in tight cliques like we do at school, or do they barely know each other's names?

I spot Franny immediately in a pale pink sweater with her long white hair pulled up in a bun on top of her head. Her eyes remind me of the color of the pale green sea glass that I used to collect along Lake Erie. When she smiles and waves at me, it's all gums—no teeth—like a newborn baby.

I decide that, if there were tables on risers looking over the others at the nursing home like there are in our school cafeteria, Franny would be the queen of them all, only a kinder, gentler queen. One who doesn't bite!

"Hi Franny Bananny," I say, smiling and putting the tray down in front of her as I pat her back. "How're you doing today?"

She smiles. "Fine, thank you, darling."

As the other nurse's aides enter the commons area to help with the lunchtime feeding, Mom sits down next to Franny and puts a tray in front of tiny Rita, who's snoring quietly, chin resting on her chest, with a small plastic baby doll cradled in her lap.

Some residents still feed themselves, but most need help and others have totally lost their will to eat anything at all. Who can blame them? I vow next time I visit I'll sneak them a candy bar or potato chips and perk up their palates.

"Gramps is on the third floor," Mom says, in between feeding spoonfuls of canned pears to Rita.

"Here? This third floor?" I jump up, almost toppling Franny's tray of food onto her lap.

"Oh, dear," Franny says. "She hops like a bunny."

"Sorry, Franny." I quickly straighten her meal and turn to Mom. "I thought he was still in the hospital. When did they move him? Why the third floor?" Everyone knows the third floor is for patients who need intensive care, the worst cases.

"He arrived early this morning. He's not . . . Jo? Jo, come back here!" she calls after me.

I'm on my way to the elevators and refuse to turn around. I stand there repeatedly pushing the *up* button as if that will make the doors open quicker.

When they finally do open, the elevator's crowded with elderly people in wheelchairs. One woman wearing an old wedding veil shouts in a quivering voice, "Make way, make way, the bridal procession is coming through!"

I step back impatiently as she clanks by with her walker. The three on wheels follow right behind her like baby ducklings.

The last woman in line pauses and reaches up to me from

her wheelchair with outstretched arms. "How about a hug, honey?" she asks in a gravelly voice.

I hesitate, wanting to sidestep her and jump on the elevator before the door closes, but I find myself reluctantly bending down for an embrace. Her hair smells like it needs a shampoo. In her lap are sugar packets, a tattered straw purse, and plastic rosary beads.

The door closes.

"Sweet girl," she says, patting my hand. She slowly wheels herself away to catch up with her friends.

I take a deep breath, feeling more relaxed as I watch her unhurried progress across the lobby. I call for the elevator again and wait in front of the doors wondering why Mom didn't want me to see Gramps.

I have my answer as soon as I enter his room. He's in bed with his eyes closed and his mouth open. He doesn't look anything like Gramps, his pale face slack and expressionless. For a moment, I panic, thinking he's dead.

But then I hear a whisper of a snore and see his chest slowly rise and fall beneath the covers.

Why are they letting him sleep when it's almost noon? Gramps was always the first one to get up in the mornings— sometimes as early as 5:30 so he could watch the sunrise and refill our birdfeeders by the kitchen window. At this rate, he's going to miss sunset.

I yank the cord on the metal blinds and the bright sunlight reflecting off the snow comes streaming through the windows. I watch tiny dust particles illuminated by the light dancing around Gramps's tired face.

Pulling up a chair, I sit there quietly waiting, but the warm sunshine doesn't wake him.

I notice the black wheels on the bottom of the bed frame and the straps that confine him in the bed. Would anybody stop me if I wheeled Gramps into the elevator and out the front door, down Clifton Boulevard and all the way home?

Lightly, I touch the top of his hand. The skin looks almost transparent and feels as fragile as the tissue paper Taryn hung in my locker. A plastic hospital bracelet with his name and ID number leaves an ugly purple bruise on his wrist. I fight the urge to squeeze his hand and wake him, yet I desperately want to see Gramps smile at me and hear his voice.

He needs his sleep, I tell myself. But I know the real reason I don't wake him is that I'm afraid. If he opens his eyes and looks into my face, will he see his Jo, or will a total stranger be sitting beside his bed?

I loosen Jim's red bandana from around my neck and tie it to the metal bedrail so when Gramps wakes up he'll have something cheerful to look at and he'll know we were here and that we care.

"I love you," I whisper, and hope that he can hear me in his dreams.

On the slow elevator ride down, I can't stop thinking about him tied in his bed. I know it's for safety, but it's humiliating. How can Mom allow Gramps to stay in a place like this? Why can't he come home?

I don't go into the commons room to say good-bye to Mom when I leave. I stride right past the fish tank, plastic flowers, and the elevator bride nagging poor

Charlotte for rice to throw at her imaginary wedding.

The winter sun in Gramps's room was deceiving. It's bitter cold outside and it freezes the tears on my cheeks and makes my face feel taut and masklike. I walk home wishing I had hockey practice today so I could feel the pleasure of crashing into something, anything, just as long as it hurts.

Today is garbage collection and Mrs. Stritch's ancient metal garbage cans are lined up in a row at the end of her driveway. Before I can stop myself, my foot makes solid contact and sends the containers clattering onto the sidewalk, rolling all over the place, spewing a week's worth of rotting trash.

Instantly, the front door opens and Mrs. Stritch appears, hands on hips, standing on her porch next to that stupid goose, which is dressed as Abraham Lincoln for President's Day. "Is that you, Joanna Giordano?" she crows.

I'm tempted to yell, "No!" and make a run for it, but suddenly I'm embarrassed by the disgusting mess I've made.

Mrs. Stritch makes her way down the steps, her spindly legs covered in thick flesh-colored knee-highs and her orange hair rolled in spongy pink curlers.

"I'm sorry, Mrs. Stritch." I kneel down and begin picking up the garbage.

"You better be sorry, you careless, clumsy girl!" she scolds as she stands over me surveying the smelly litter.

"I tripped . . . accidentally-on-purpose," I mumble, but Mrs. Stritch is not listening as she points out every last eggshell, chicken bone, and stinky cat food can.

"You could recycle these, Mrs. Stritch," I offer, holding up the aluminum tins.

"Mind your own bee's wax!" she yelps.

I jump, trying to gather the debris faster.

In her next breath, she says, "So I hear your grandfather's in the hospital."

"Actually, he's at the nursing home."

"Oh, I'm so surprised," she says, making a *tsk-tsk*ing sound with her tongue and pulling her flowered housecoat tighter around her neck.

Isn't she freezing? Or are witches cold-blooded?

"I would have thought your mother, with all her work experience, would have taken care of her father at home," Mrs. Stritch says. She points to a few soggy teabags I missed.

I decide she must have an icicle up her butt and she definitely hasn't forgiven Gramps for the goose-napping incident. "Aren't you freezing, Mrs. Stritch?" I ask. "You don't want to catch pneumonia."

She glares at me, then inspects her sidewalk and driveway. "Watch where you're walking *accidentally-on-purpose* next time, young lady." She turns and retreats back inside, where she'll sit by the front window, her head full of pink foam, keeping watch over her silly goose and rusty trash cans.

I swish my filthy hands in the snow and dry them with my scarf. My fingers are red and plumped up from the cold, looking like sausages. "Feel better now, Jo?" I say out loud, with a disappointed sigh.

I'll wait until I'm in front of Ben's house before crossing over to my side of the street. I'm hoping he might be outside. Most Saturdays, his father makes him help wash, wax, and vacuum their cars, even in the dead of winter. "Helps remove the salt from the snowplows that can destroy a car's outer shell if allowed to sit for over seventy-two hours," Ben once dutifully explained to me in mocking imitation of his father.

I remember when we were kids, Ben accidentally scraped the handlebar of his bicycle against the side of his dad's blue Buick. From his father's reaction, you would have thought Ben had taken a sledgehammer to the hood. As Mr. McCloud applied two coats of touch-up paint and buffed and waxed the grazed spot, he lectured Ben on respecting property, especially "Big Blue." Mr. McCloud names his cars.

I'm pretty sure that the only wax my dad's cars have ever seen was Michael's forgotten crayons that melted into the seats on hot summer days.

The McClouds' garage is closed, no sign of Ben. I remember his smile after he scored the first goal last night. I want to ask him how his shoulder's doing and when he'll be able to skate again, but I don't dare ring the doorbell or call on the phone. What if Mr. McCloud answers?

I should go inside and write that current events article due in health class on Monday. But as I climb the steps to let myself in, I hear the Christmas lights scraping against the gutters. In the past, it's always been Dad's job to take the decorations down after the holidays.

I push the plug into the socket and the house lights up in a multicolor blinking display. So it looks a little weird in the middle of the afternoon, weeks after Christmas has come and gone, but it gives me stubborn hope, which is about all I've got to hang on to right now, unless you count a reindeer's blinking red nose.

Nine

*I*n health class, we're studying "growth and development," which is just another name for sex education. Mr. Gadlock has been teaching middle school health for over thirty years and he takes his job very seriously. "What you learn in this class could mean the difference between life and death," he informs us on the first day.

And if that doesn't grab our attention, the full-body skeleton hanging in the corner and a hundred slides containing graphic pictures of sexual diseases certainly will.

"Make smart choices!" he preaches.

The funny thing is that, every year, Gadlock chooses to be absent the week he's scheduled to explain the details of human reproduction to his classes. When the sex talk comes around, you can pretty much count on entering the health classroom and seeing a nervous substitute teacher, paralyzed in front of the chalkboard, wearing a deer-caught-in-the-headlights expression on her face.

They fumble with Gadlock's ancient notes, trying to get up the nerve to say words like "gonads" and "erection" in front of seventh graders whose hormones are running wild 24/7.

Today, I picture Gadlock kickin' back in some trendy coffee shop, listening to jazz music and congratulating himself on once again having skipped the sex talk. As for the substitute, they won't pay her nearly enough for the pain and suffering she'll endure before the final bell rings.

I feel sorry for her because she looks young and carries a serious-looking briefcase, hopefully filled with aspirin and duct tape for keeping students in their seats, mouths shut.

She tries to teach the lesson, but it's no use. Derek trips her up every step of the way.

Miss Sub (friendly smile—big mistake): "Class, please take out your books."

Derek (matching smile): "Hey, you look too young to teach. How old are you anyway?"

Miss Sub (charmed, dodges the question, still smiling): "Now, let's open to page ten and will someone please begin reading about (clears throat) the male reproductive system."

Derek (hand raised): "Have a boyfriend?"

Miss Sub (smile fading fast): "That's a personal question (glances at the seating chart), Mark! (Derek's in the wrong seat.) Now, let's get back to the lesson."

Derek (closing in for the kill): "Have sex with your boyfriend?"

Miss Sub (Panic! Alarm! Definitely not smiling): "Mark! I'm going to send you to the office if you continue with these inappropriate questions."

Derek (satisfied grin, because everyone knows she's afraid to send him to the office, otherwise he would have been there already. Besides, it would make her look like she's lost control of the class, which she never had in the first place): "Hey, it's sex ed, right? Our history teacher says primary sources are best."

Miss Sub abandons the lesson and retreats behind Gadlock's desk in order to reread a manual Lubic issued her in the office, *Everything You Always Wanted to Know about Substitute Teaching but Were Afraid to Ask*. My guess is that right now, she's looking up the procedure on how to obtain a sub for the sub.

Anyway, there's really nothing that she can teach us from a textbook, unless it gives advice on how to avoid the empty classrooms during a school dance where stuff that got President Clinton in trouble has been rumored to take place, or how to tell your parents that the gym teacher creeps you out when he puts his hand on your shoulder and says that he can see that you're an athlete because you have great legs. Or maybe there's a chapter in there on how to deal with the boys who "accidentally" brush against your chest or try to grab your butt in the crowded hallways at school.

I give her a "P" for persistence, though, because with only ten minutes left in class, she's back on her feet, determined to give it one more try. "Class, it's time for the health current event reports."

Derek's hand is up first, and you'd think she'd learned her lesson. Nope—change that to a "D" for just plain "dumb," as she points to Derek and says, "Go ahead, Mark. You may go first."

Maybe she believes in forgiveness and redemption, but I have no pity for her.

Derek stands up in front of the room and actually does a pretty good job of summarizing his article on childhood obesity. He gives the reasons it seems to be on the rise and even points out that the deals many schools make with the cola and vending machine companies tempt kids into eating only junk food, while fruits and veggies brought from home are slam-dunked in the cafeteria garbage cans daily.

Derek begins to cross the line when he mentions that in Arkansas, kids receive health report cards from their schools and that if they're overweight, they get a letter grade of "F"— for "fat."

He pauses for a moment to let the laughter die down and then announces, "And that's just what we need here!"

Derek begins reading the names of people he'd rate as an "F" on the fat scale at our school.

I can feel my hands sweat. I'm not overweight, so I shouldn't care about Derek's stupid list, but I know he wouldn't hesitate to put people on it just for a joke and a laugh.

"That's enough, Mark!" Miss Sub tries to cut him off, but she gave him the floor and he's not about to relinquish it.

Derek drones on in a serious voice, reading out loud a long list that, besides students, also includes teachers, the superintendent, and a cafeteria lady or two. The class goes wild, howling, laughing, pounding on the desks with each new name read.

When Valerie hears her name, she leaps out of her seat and screeches, "I'm not fat!"

She knows that Derek's only teasing her, but she's going to play this scene for all it's worth.

"Turn around!" he orders her.

Valerie does a slow twirl and he whistles admiringly at her butt in tight jeans, and the white T-shirt that barely covers her pierced navel and shows off her ample chest.

Derek smacks his hand to his head and says, "Whoa, Val! You have been officially transferred to the Hot List."

Derek's friends in the back of the room are going crazy, chairs are tipping over, people are climbing out of their seats.

"Quiet! Quiet right this minute!" shrieks Miss Sub.

It has no effect on the noise level. I glance across the room at Ben to see if he's enjoying the show. His head is down and he's writing something on a piece of loose-leaf paper. Is he upset because Derek's flirting with Valerie? Or is he thinking of his mother, who is one of the nicest people on our block but probably weighs over two hundred pounds?

Derek has pushed the sub to the limit. She opens her briefcase like she means business and waves an Office Incident Report in front of the class. She checks the seating chart one last time and fills out the report on Mark Nussbaum, a straight-A student who has never missed a day of school or gotten in trouble before in his life. Meanwhile, Derek continues the roll call.

"For a small fee," he says, "I offer my services as a personal trainer to help F-List people improve their grades. Maybe bring them up to a 'P' for 'pudgy.'"

The bell rings. Show's over. As we file out of the classroom, Derek winks at Miss Sub and says, "Hey, nothing personal."

"Thanks, Mark," she says and slams her briefcase closed.

✳✳✳

Between classes, I stop to check if my locker's been fixed. I can still see a little scrap of red tissue paper sticking out of the vents. I turn the combination and voila! It pops open.

Inside, there's a memo on official school paper taped to the door. *Defacing school property is against Board of Education policy. All violators will be prosecuted. See Student Handbook, page 32, section 8c.*

I rip the notice down, crumple the paper, and toss it to the bottom of the locker.

I admire Taryn's artistic design again and wish everything in my life were this colorful and organized. "Oops," I say out loud and bend over to pick up the paper I just pitched. "Organized locker, organized life."

Running my fingers along the wind chimes hanging on the coat hook, they make a sound that reminds me of fairies and elves dancing in an enchanted forest. Suddenly, I have a better idea. I unhook the chimes and put them in my backpack.

Principal Lubic is patrolling the hall and stops in front of my locker. "Great game on Friday, young lady," he says.

"Thanks." I stand tall, hoping to block his view of the inside. He probably wouldn't appreciate Taryn's artistic efforts, considering his clutterless desk and his devotion to the student handbook.

Who am I kidding? I'm barely five feet tall on my skates. At that moment, I notice a folded-up sheet of notebook paper wedged into the vent on my locker door.

"It's what we encourage around here," Lubic says, gazing a little above my right shoulder, "every learner pursuing his —or her—talents to the fullest."

Is he complimenting Taryn's decorating or my hockey skills? I shrug, figuring "Thanks" is a safe response either way.

The bell rings.

I grab the note and slam the locker closed, giving it a hard check with my right shoulder and ignoring Lubic's is-that-how-we-treat-school-property look.

"Just practicing," I tell him as I race down the hall to English.

Ms. Freeman just looks up and nods when I slip into my seat a minute late. Today we're supposed to run through the play, but someone has her off and running on a heated political discussion about dictators and petty tyrants.

Sometimes I think kids ask questions knowing exactly what topics will get individual teachers sidetracked. It's just a game to avoid covering the work planned for that day. For some teachers, it's as easy as bringing up the latest football scores. For others, like Ms. Freeman, there has to be at least some educational value in the digression.

Carefully, I unwrap the tightly folded note in the palm of my hand and immediately recognize the handwriting.

Jo, meet me after practice. Ben
P.S. My shoulder's sprained and I'm going to miss a couple
of games.

I know I should feel sad about Ben's not being able to play hockey, but instead I'm happy, rereading over and over again the sentence about meeting after practice.

What does he want to talk to me about? We haven't

walked home together in so long I can hardly wait for the end of the day.

"Jo, up here, please!"

"Sorry, Ms. Freeman." I quickly hide the note in my binder and open my textbook to Act III, scene I of *Julius Caesar*.

Valerie's still yapping about wearing white togas for the performance, and Derek's questioning her on what she plans to wear underneath her toga.

I remember that after practice I was going to stop at the nursing home to see how Gramps is doing. I wonder if Ben would mind coming in with me.

"Enough!" says Ms. Freeman, who, unlike Miss Sub, carries real authority without having to raise her voice. "Let's settle down. We're reading a Shakespearean play, not playing around, and if that doesn't motivate all of you, the test this Thursday certainly will."

At hockey practice, you'd think everyone would still be talking about last Friday's incredible win, well, at least Coach is, but surprisingly all the buzz concerns the upcoming Valentine's dance this weekend: who's been asked and who's been dumped, what kind of music, what to wear—and they say girls have a rep for gossiping?

Ben is sitting on the bench with his arm in a sling that secures the injured shoulder to his chest. As I walk past him to go out onto the ice for practice, I say, "See you later, Ben."

He smiles and nods, but beyond that, I can't read the expression on his face.

Even without Ben on the ice today, practice is going a little easier for me. Maybe after Friday's game-winning assist, these guys finally realize that I'm not the enemy.

Coach Granato is already talking about our next game and that some people are saying it was luck that we beat the Wildcats. "Hard work produces good luck!" he insists as we line up for shooting drills.

His enthusiasm and belief in us are contagious. For the first time in a long while, I feel happy and worry-free out here, enjoying the tired ache in my muscles and feeling like part of the team.

After practice is through, I take a little longer than usual changing, combing my hair in the locker room mirror and applying some lip gloss. I'm torn between hope that Ben's waiting for me and fear that he changed his mind and decided to walk home with the guys after all.

I shouldn't doubt him.

As promised, he's standing outside the locker room door bouncing a fuzzy yellow tennis ball against the wall and catching it with his good arm.

He misses when he looks up at me and the ball *pitter-patters* down the hallway. "I was beginning to wonder if you'd snuck out the back," he says.

"No, I just had a lot of things to get together. Sorry about the shoulder, Ben."

"It's okay, doctor says I might be back in a week." He rubs the shoulder lightly. "Hey, listen, Jo, I guess you're probably angry with me . . . these last few weeks have been really hard."

My heart's pounding. "I'm not mad at you, Ben." Okay, I'm lying. Maybe I'm a *little* mad, but I'm not going to admit it now.

"This whole hockey thing . . . and you making the team and all, it's really confusing."

We've caught up with the tennis ball, and he reaches down and scoops it up.

The exit doors that lead to the parking lot are in front of us when I notice he's not wearing a coat or carrying his books.

"Do you need to go to your locker to get your stuff before we walk home?" I ask.

Shrieks of laughter echo from down the hallway. The cheerleaders are painting big red hearts on wide rolls of white paper.

Ben looks embarrassed for a minute and gives that half shrug I know so well. "Actually, I'm staying after to help with the decorations . . . for the dance."

"Hey, Benny! Get your butt back here," Heather calls. "We need height to hang these up."

Valerie, dressed in skimpy shorts that reveal her long, chemically tanned legs, breaks away from her friends and begins to walk toward us, calling down the hallway, "Come on, Ben!"

Ben looks embarrassed, turning to Valerie and then back to me. He leans against the metal bar on the door, but I push past him. "I got it," I say.

"Jo, wait a minute!"

Don't turn around, I tell myself. I can't believe I was so

stupid to think that things could magically go back to how they were before. Now that he's hanging with Valerie and Derek, why would he give up popularity to be with me?

"Jo!"

I keep walking. From inside the school I hear, "Benny!" and seconds later, the sound of the metal doors clicking closed.

I sneak a look back over my shoulder. He's gone. "Help hang decorations! Yeah, right, with one arm?" I say out loud.

Still, I fight the urge to turn around and march back in there to tell Ben that he should be walking home with me and not wasting his time hanging paper hearts with a fluff chick like Valerie. I want to tell him that I've missed him and that it stinks that he's sidelined from hockey for a while. I want to talk to him about Gramps, Jim, and my dad.

And before I know it, I'm heading back toward the door. I'm not a quitter.

I don't have my gloves on yet, so my hand burns when it touches the metal door handle. I yank it toward me, but it doesn't budge.

Locked out.

No way back inside unless I pound on the door and shout, "Open up!"

I shove my freezing hands into my pockets, turn, and head down the icy sidewalk. "I'm not a quitter, but I still have some pride."

Ten

It's dark by the time I reach the nursing home. Gramps is sitting up in bed wearing Jim's red bandana tied on top of his head.

"Hey, looking good, Gramps." I lean over and give him a kiss on his cheek. Dropping my backpack and hockey bag on the floor, I sit down on the edge of the bed and take his hand in mine.

He smiles and nods. I wonder if it's an automatic response or if he really recognizes me.

"Have you seen Mom?" I ask.

He stares at me with a blank expression.

"Oh, sorry, Gramps, I mean my mom, your daughter, Jean. Has she been here yet?"

Without warning, he suddenly looks upset. Pointing outside toward the nursing station, he mumbles, "Doing this . . . doing that." He pulls his hand from mine and makes agitated movements across his bedsheets.

Finally, he gives up and shakes his head, sighing. "Can't, can't . . . peddle the bus with . . . goobly-goop there." He looks at me with an expression of relief at finally getting his thoughts out.

My turn.

Isn't that the way conversation is supposed to go? Give and take, back and forth, building meaning, making connections. Only I have no idea what Gramps and I are building, and I'm afraid if I don't hold up my end of the conversation, the whole thing will collapse around us.

"Sure, Gramps," I say softly, picking at the nubs of lint on his bedspread, "you can't peddle the bus with all that goobly-goop."

But the minute the words are out, I feel like it's a betrayal of the smart, funny man I once knew.

How long, I wonder, has Gramps not been making sense? Or did it just all fall apart that night in the bathroom? I've been so busy worrying about my own stupid problems that I guess I really hadn't taken the time to notice just how confused he was becoming.

Suddenly, I remembered the index cards with the names of rooms and ordinary household objects written on them. It was so weird walking around the house and finding these white cards naming everything, taped to objects and doors: "light switch," "refrigerator," "coat closet," "bathroom," "sofa."

Mom had taped them everywhere this summer, explaining that they would help Michael learn his sight words for reading. Maybe that was it, or maybe the name cards were reminders for Gramps, helping him hold on to words and their meanings just a little bit longer.

I feel the tears welling up in my eyes. Michael and Gramps, best buddies passing each other by—one on the way up and the other on the way down—and me, impatient with both of them.

"Hey, Gramps." I wipe my eyes with the back of my hand and then unzip my backpack. "Look what I brought you."

I pull out the wind chimes that Taryn gave me and hang them from the IV stand over his bed. The tinkling sounds of the icicle-like chimes fill the room. Gramps smiles.

"My friend gave them to me for my locker. They're supposed to bring good luck."

For the next hour, I sit next to him and spill my heart out. I tell Gramps about Jim's surprise visit to watch my first game and how we beat the top-ranked team. I hold his hand and admire the thick gold US Air Force pilot ring from WWII that he wears on his right ring finger.

Incredibly, for a brief moment, he tells me about one of his missions flying B-24 Liberators in the South Pacific. How does he remember the type of plane he flew and not his own address or our names?

My hopes soar that he'll get better and will come home soon. But, then, in the very next sentence, he's speaking gibberish again and looking to me to throw him a lifeline, and all I have to offer is my hand and a meaningless story of my own about how my locker got jammed at school.

A nurse's aide comes into the room carrying a dinner tray. I lift the metal warming lid and say, "Gramps, doesn't this look delicious?"

He leans over and peers at the plate. "Pile of crap," he says.

I laugh so hard I almost fall off the edge of the bed.

After I finish helping him with his meal, I take the elevator downstairs to look for Mom. I find her in a patient's room changing someone's diaper, and I have to walk out of the room to stop myself from gagging.

Mom calls to me in a teasing voice, "Jo, if you throw up, you clean up. I've got enough work around here!"

"Sorry, Mom. I'm just not good with that kind of stuff. How do you do it?"

"Hey, I did it for you, didn't I?" she says. "And there was no paycheck involved."

"Yeah, but I was a baby and had baby-sized poo."

She laughs, "Poo is poo, honey, no matter what size."

Mom wheels tiny Rita and her baby doll into the commons room and gets her ready for dinner.

Across the room, people have gathered around Franny. A slim, stylish woman dressed in a silk suit and high heels is holding a large helium balloon that says *Happy Birthday!* Franny sits there, smiling her toothless grin, wearing a big bow and holding a fancy gift-wrapped box on her lap. A large bouquet of yellow roses rests on the table next to Franny's meal tray.

Hiding behind the bouquet is Valerie Holm.

We recognize each other at the exact same moment. She looks flustered, turning away and refusing to look at me.

After Franny opens her present, a beautiful pale blue sweater, and takes a couple of bites of the vanilla-frosted cake, the party's over and her company begins to gather their things to leave.

I watch the woman in the suit bend over and give Franny

a quick peck on the cheek. "Happy birthday, Mom," she says, while Valerie gives Franny a hug and kisses the air next to her ear.

Franny, in the middle, holds on to both of their hands.

As they leave, mother and daughter cautiously maneuver their way around the other patients parked in wheelchairs in front of the tables.

Impulsively, I head toward a cutoff point to intercept them before they escape.

"Hi, Valerie!"

They stop, and the tall woman checks me out from head to toe, taking in the wild hair, sweatpants, and sneakers.

Valerie mumbles, "Hi," and quickly glances toward the door in the lobby.

Switching her designer handbag to her other arm, the woman looks at her daughter expectantly. "Valerie?"

"Sorry. This is Jo, from school. Jo, this is my mother."

Valerie's mom extends her tan, manicured hand, which sparkles with diamonds as big as icebergs. "Call me Margo. Nice to meet you, Jo." She pumps my hand twice. "Do you work here?"

"No, but my mom does." I turn and point in her direction as she's coaxing Rita to eat one more spoonful of puréed carrots.

"How nice," Margo says. "It's good to know someone personally to leave instructions with about my mother's care. I'm not happy with the way they've been styling her hair lately. Very unbecoming."

Automatically, the three of us turn to look at Franny,

who is enjoying the sensation of rubbing her new birthday sweater against her cheek.

I want to tell Valerie's mom, "Franny's hair is fine the way it is. Who cares how it's styled, just as long as it's clean? And besides, look around, lady, most of the people in this place are bald—at least Franny has hair!"

But I bite my tongue and just nod, mumbling, "I'll give her the message."

"You're such a help. And could you also inform her that I've put another bottle of body lotion on my mother's dresser in her room? Her skin's so dry in the winter. It's very expensive cream, so I'd appreciate it if it's used sparingly and only for my mother. The last bottle disappeared in less than two months!"

"Maybe you'd better inform her yourself." I point out Mom again across the room.

I watch Margo walk over, sidestepping the outstretched hands of a patient who reaches for her and calls, "Mama?"

Valerie and I are left standing there.

Maybe I'm feeling brave because she's out of her element and clearly uncomfortable, while I feel right at home, because for the first time ever, I begin a conversation with Valerie Holm. "Franny's your grandmother?" I ask.

Valerie nods and looks over at Franny. "She used to live in a big old house up on Briar Cliff Lane. I'd sleep over there every Friday night when I was a little girl, but then she fell and broke her hip." Valerie's eyes begin to fill with tears. "They put her in here to recover, but that was over three years ago. . . ."

I can't believe that Valerie, queen of seventh grade, is actually talking to me like a normal person, no put-downs or sarcastic comments. And I know exactly how she feels, because I feel the same way about Gramps being in here. Tentatively, I reach out and touch Valerie's arm. "Franny's one of our favorites," I tell her. "We really love her."

Valerie pushes me away. "You love her?" she snaps. "You don't even know her. She's *my* grandmother!"

My face burns as if she'd just slapped it.

"I mean . . . ," I say, but I can't think of anything to describe how I feel.

"You're not moving in on my grandmother, Jo Giordano, just like you moved in on the boys' hockey team. No way," Valerie says and then turns her back on me, striding toward her mother.

I stand there in shock staring at Franny and feeling the heat slowly drain from my face. How can kind Franny and cruel Valerie be related? Maybe Valerie will mellow as she grows older. But at this rate, she'd have to live over a century to acquire even a tenth of her grandmother's sweetness.

At least now I know where those comments about using nursing-home sheets for togas came from. Valerie had been here before; maybe she'd even watched my mother taking care of Franny.

I study my mom in her polyester uniform and thick-soled sneakers. What a contrast compared to Margo, standing there looking like she just stepped out of an expensive clothing catalog, writing a list of instructions in a tiny pink notebook with a matching silver pen.

I walk over and stand behind Mom and Rita. Margo tears off the sheets of paper and hands them to Mom. Then she turns her attention to me and asks, "Are you planning to attend the Valentine's dance this Saturday at school?"

Before I answer, she continues, "Valerie and I are on our way to the mall to pick out new outfits. She's been so busy with cheerleading for two sports this winter—basketball and hockey. Plus, she's head of the decorating committee for the dance, and me with all my PTA and Junior League volunteering, well, we can hardly find time to shop together anymore!"

At that moment, Rita farts so loud and long that it sounds like a foghorn guiding lost ships to shore.

Valerie and her mother take two baby steps backward, as if they're playing the game "Mother May I?" in reverse.

"Scusi," Rita mumbles as she shifts in her chair and hugs her baby doll closer.

"You're excused, Rita," Mom says with a smile, as we watch Valerie and Margo beat a hasty retreat through the lobby.

"So she cheers for two sports?" Mom asks, as she gathers up the dishes and puts them on the tray.

I shrug. "I never notice them when I'm skating."

"Funny, I've never noticed them, either." Mom collects the trays to load onto the cart, which will be wheeled back down to the kitchen after everyone is finished eating.

Suddenly, she reaches over and rubs my back. "I'm glad you're out there skating, Jo. Both your father and I are—"

I hold up my hand. "Not Dad, okay? He ruins everything for me."

"You should return his calls—"

"What for? It's the same old excuses and promises. I don't want to see him, and especially not at any of my games. It's hard enough playing without worrying about what crazy thing he'll dream up next to embarrass me."

Mom's shoulders slump a little and she sighs, "You don't mean that, Jo." She looks so tired that I feel guilty for putting her in the middle.

"Hey, Mom, you weren't at the game, okay? Why don't you just divorce him already? I wouldn't be sad. I wouldn't blame you. No one would."

Ignoring my comments, she finishes stacking the trays. She searches for her time card in her purse as we make our way to the lobby. She slips the card into the slot at the top of an old industrial-sized clock. It eats the card in a quick metallic gulp and spits it back out with a red "7:05 P.M." printed next to today's date.

Together we walk through the darkened lobby, past the bubbling fish tanks with their iridescent glow, stopping at the glass doors with a thousand fingerprints revealed through the streetlight's backlighting. But Mom goes no farther.

"I need to run upstairs to check on Gramps for a little bit. You head home and I'll be there soon," she says.

"Mom, I saw Gramps when I got here. He's doing fine." Then I tell her about the WWII stories, feeling guilty because I'm hoping she'll change her mind and walk home with me.

"I'll only be a minute," she says. She tugs my collar up around my neck. "Your father's dropping Michael off in a half hour, so I need you at home."

"Please, Mom, come on." I grab her hand, feeling like I'm back in kindergarten, afraid to walk into school alone on the first day.

She sighs and kisses the top of my head. "It's not far. You're a big girl, Jo. Reheat the macaroni and cheese, and I'll be home soon."

Watching her push the elevator button, I make sure I'm wearing the most pitiful expression on my face, hoping to guilt her into changing her mind. I stand there watching as she steps inside and gives me a quick wave, and wait until the door closes before I admit defeat.

Outside, I curse out loud and kick a chunk of ice, watching it skid across the parking lot, hit a hubcap, and shatter into a hundred little pieces. "Sure, I can walk home alone! But do I want to? Does anybody care?"

I think of Ben's standing me up at the gym door earlier this evening, and now even my own mother turns away. I unzip my jacket and take a quick sniff under my arms. "Do I stink or something?"

And what's waiting for me? Dark house. Leftovers. Dad! Gee, I feel like skipping the rest of the way home. I'll get there quicker.

I vow to take a very long shower, the kind that empties the hot-water tank and shrivels your body until you look like a California raisin. With any luck, Dad will leave his truck running, deposit Michael on the front steps, ring the doorbell, and then run away like some Halloween trickster.

But even I know the sad truth. When it comes to my father, you can definitely count on more tricks than treats.

Eleven

The next morning in Ms. Freeman's class, everyone is running around in bare feet and bedsheets, frantically trying to get ready for *Julius Caesar*, which we're scheduled to perform in front of the sixth graders in fifteen minutes.

For once, Valerie didn't get her wish—no white togas. Instead, there's everything from plaid to paisley, pinstripes to cartoon characters. Valerie, however, wears white satin sheets, spiked heels, and a rhinestone tiara on top of her head. "All hail Caesar!" she proclaims as she struts her stuff around the classroom.

Ms. Freeman advises her to make a few adjustments to her toga. "Caesar need not display any cleavage or belly button jewelry," she informs Valerie.

Valerie complains and Derek accuses Ms. Freeman of censorship, then he notices my outfit and says, "Nice toga, Giordano!"

I'm wrapped in Michael's *Sesame Street* sheets, with one of Gramps's old striped ties, smelling faintly of mothballs, belted around my waist.

Although Valerie doesn't have the most lines in the play,

she prolongs her moment in the spotlight by reciting every last word slowly and with great emphasis. The rest of us speak our parts a little too quickly, and even though it's only a captive audience of sixth graders, I can tell that no one wants to forget their lines and stand there onstage with a brain freeze.

Fortunately, it happened only once—to Derek, who plays Mark Antony, and he just ad-libbed his way through it as easily as he skates around obstacles on the ice, confident that he'll find his way out of any jam and make it work to his advantage.

At the climax of the play, when Caesar is murdered in the Senate, I stab my fake dagger into Valerie a little too hard, because she squeals, "Ouch, that hurt!"

The audience laughs. Valerie remembers her real lines and asks, "Et tu, Brute?" and then crawls around the stage gasping and clutching at her heart.

Give me a break! Ms. Freeman was right when she told us, "Poorly acted tragedy is comic."

After five minutes, and some stern looks from Ms. Freeman, Valerie finally croaks and Caesar's dead body is supposed to be carried offstage. Only, Derek accidentally steps on Valerie's toga as he's dragging her away, pulling it from her body and revealing to the entire sixth grade that, unlike the rest of the cast, Valerie chose to ignore Ms. Freeman's requirement that shorts and tank tops be worn under all togas.

Shock and awe.

It was, without a doubt, the most flagrant dress code

violation in the history of public schools. Which consequently landed Valerie Holm an interview with Principal Lubic immediately following the final curtain call.

Of course, Valerie didn't get into any trouble for flashing an auditorium full of preteens. As she tells it, she gave an Oscar-worthy performance sitting in the principal's office, crying about how embarrassed she was and how she would never be able to show her face in school again.

Lubic stood there patting her shoulder and telling her not to worry, because—drum roll, please—"In this school, nothing stands in the way of every learner pursuing their talents to the fullest!"

I wonder what talent he had in mind for Valerie—future Victoria's Secret model?

After the play, I peek into the gym. The cheerleaders are setting up for the Valentine's Dance tomorrow night. They're buzzing around, taping red construction-paper hearts to everything: walls, doors, basketball hoops, and bleachers.

For two weeks before the dance, the cheerleaders sold these hearts during lunch periods, two for a dollar, and you could write any message you wanted to on them.

Taryn actually came up with the bright idea that I should give Ben one, so I bought two hearts, just in case I messed one up. I've been testing possible messages out in my head, from the boring, *Ben, let's be friends!* to the rhythmically challenged, *Roses are red, violets are blue. Ben McCloud, I miss you!*

Gag me.

And so, my blank paper hearts are stuffed in my feng shui locker bringing very little harmony and happiness into my life. In fact, every time I look at them, I'm miserable. I mean, I'm not exactly sure that a message on a Valentine is the right message for Ben.

At lunch, it's still just Taryn and I battling for nutritional and social survival in the mosh pit. Without Gramps making my sandwiches, the adventure of eating lunch is definitely over. Gone are the prune-and-yogurt mixes, the raisin and Swiss cheese sandwiches, and the frozen broccoli sprinkled with cinnamon.

Here to stay are the PB&J sandwiches that I slap together for myself at 6 A.M. and toss into a brown bag with an apple, which inevitably smashes a soggy jelly dent in the middle of the sandwich.

Taryn never considers my lunch when she's scoping the tables for a trade.

At least I know now where Ben is hiding out. Taryn told me that a friend of hers saw him eating lunch at the library. When she asked him what he was working on, he said, "History project."

The way things are going between us, I think it's going to be a long-term project, one that lasts the entire school year.

If I were the librarian, Ms. Elliott, I'd be suspicious by early May when Ben's more than halfway through the text-book. Everyone knows we never make it past the New Deal before the school year ends, and come September, we're right back to the Niña, Pinta, and Santa Maria all over again.

It's educational déjà vu, and then miraculously, one day we'll dress in shower-curtain-like robes (will Valerie wear anything underneath?) and march across the stage to receive a diploma declaring us competent, at least by state minimum standards.

Ms. Freeman wasn't kidding when she spoke about the cyclical nature of things. It's just that sometimes I wish I could just step off and let the rest of the world cycle on by.

Maybe I'd be doing Ben a favor if I got in his face and said, "Listen up, McCloud, are we going to keep avoiding each other for the rest of our lives, or are we going to settle this thing once and for all?"

I shudder as I crush my paper lunch bag into a ball. It's scary just how much I'm beginning to sound like my father. Could it be genetic?

Second-to-last period of the day and Ms. Freeman doesn't even pretend that she's going to accomplish much. Everybody's talking about our performance earlier and, of course, Valerie's grand reveal. Besides, with the dance tomorrow night, there's frenzied gossip on who's going out and who's been dumped.

All Ms. Freeman can do is attempt to cover some basic grammar. Unfortunately, grammar is the one area of English that's similar to déjà vu history.

Every year, we read new novels and write on different topics, but we can't seem to escape reviewing basic parts of speech over and over again. If we can't recognize a noun, verb, or adjective, then it's a safe bet that we can kiss any hope of AP English good-bye.

Looking around the room, I feel sorry for Ms. Freeman. We're a pretty pathetic bunch.

Derek's asleep, long strings of drool pooling on his spiral notebook.

Valerie's passing notes.

Heather's writing on her hands in pen the answers to the Spanish test she takes next period.

Angelo stutters a little as he reads out loud a sentence from our grammar book and then tries to name the prepositional phrases.

I overhear Valerie whisper to Courtney, "Lucky Angelo has the word 'Italy' written in the middle of his tattoo or he'd forget what country it is."

I want to tell her to shut up, that Angelo may have trouble saying some words, but he's smart and he's got a good heart. I remember when we were in the fifth grade and a group of kids were mimicking a deaf boy, Jamie, because of the funny way he spoke. Angelo came to his defense and threatened to beat the crap out of anyone if they ever teased Jamie again.

Angelo isn't the biggest kid in the school, but there's something fierce and brave about him, and his speaking up ended Jamie's playground tortures forever.

I hate the way Valerie looks down on Angelo, Jamie, and all the other kids at school who are different or who don't have money, good looks, and expensive clothes.

After he's done reading his sentence, Angelo returns to drawing the most amazing picture of battling fire-breathing dragons in his notebook, oblivious once again to the grammar lesson taking place around him.

Ms. Freeman glances my way. She's got me. I'm totally

lost and have no idea what problem we're on. But she doesn't call on me. Instead, she raises her eyebrows as if to say, *get with the program*, and then rouses Derek from his nap to read the next two sentences.

That's why she's my favorite teacher, even though I don't see how she gets so charged up over books all the time. Most of my other teachers would have been "Gotcha!"

"And . . . Jo, last two, please."

Busted. Scratch the favorite-teacher award. Nervously, I scan the page and once again, I'm clueless as to which last two sentences she means.

Valerie snickers.

I give her a dirty look.

"Got it, Ms. F.," Angelo says. He reads the sentences out loud, stumbling once or twice, but he doesn't give up until he lists the prepositions in each one.

I smile and mouth the word "thanks" to Angelo. People are always surprising you.

Angelo nods and goes back to his dragons.

My stomach feels queasy, my hands sweat, and I'm pretty sure I'm running a fever. After consulting the Internet, I diagnose malaria and explain to Mom that it would be totally irresponsible to attend the dance tonight and risk infecting my classmates.

"Malaria? In Ohio?" she asks.

Why didn't I settle for plain old stomach flu?

Mom glances up from folding the laundry but doesn't even bother to check my forehead to see if it's hot. "You don't want to go to the dance, do you?"

I shake my head and kneel down on the floor and begin matching up the socks. Surely, she'll recognize this as a sign of serious illness since I rarely pitch in to fold the clothes.

"Is it because I didn't take you shopping for a new outfit like Valerie's mom?" she asks with a smile.

"No!" I chuck a balled-up pair of socks at her head, and she ducks in time to avoid the hit.

"Because we could definitely throw something together for you," she says, as she pulls a pair of her underpants, the kind I call old lady grunders, out of the pile and slips them over her head like a hat.

"Mom!" I groan. "It's not clothes. It's, it's . . . stress."

"Stress?"

"Take those off your head. You look like Little Bo Peep. Yeah, stress," I say, hoping this diagnosis sticks.

"What does a thirteen-year-old have to be stressed about, Jo?"

"Everything—school, hockey, world peace, friends."

"Ben?" she says, nailing it. Reaching over the laundry pile, she takes the mismatched navy and black socks from my hands.

"I'm so confused. It seems like he's going to ask Valerie out. I hate the thought of it. I want him back, but I don't know if I want a boyfriend or just a friend. Every day at school, someone's going out with someone new, and then the next minute, they dump 'em. It's a game. I don't want to play it."

"Hmm, I don't know, Jo." She shakes her head. "I'm not really the best person to offer advice on this topic. I only went out with one person in high school."

"Dad?"

She nods. "We weren't even friends before we started dating. We really didn't have much in common, well, except proximity. His locker was right next to mine," she says with a crooked smile.

Suddenly, Mom looks a little sad and I regret bringing up the topic at all.

"Still, you might want to think about going to that dance tonight, Jo. You're not going to figure things out by sitting home here alone, and Taryn's counting on you to be there."

I nod my head.

"And besides," she says, "you're terrible at folding laundry."

I give her a quick kiss on the cheek and head upstairs to change.

I stand in front of my open closet trying to decide what I'm going to wear, not that there's much choice.

I think of Valerie and her mom shopping for new clothes just for one silly dance. I didn't even get to shop for new clothes at the beginning of the school year. I knew Mom couldn't afford it, and with dad in between jobs again, there just wasn't the money.

Ten minutes before Taryn's mom is supposed to pick me up for the dance, I check myself out in the bathroom mirror—gray-blue eyes, dark lashes. I wonder how Gramps looked into this same mirror and didn't recognize his own face, the one he's lived with for eighty-two years?

And yet maybe we never really see ourselves as we truly

are. At school I've watched twig-girls in the bathrooms staring at themselves in the full-length mirrors, checking out their boney butts and saying, "Oh, my God, I'm sooo fat!"

Then they vow to consume nothing but bottled water for the next two days so they can lose weight. Are they seeing the true picture?

Or take Valerie, who's so in love with her own reflection that she's had a few near collisions in the hallways because she's preoccupied with watching herself in the tinted windows of the corridors. In study hall, she spends the entire forty minutes studying her face in a compact mirror and applying makeup.

I bring my face within an inch of the glass. Gramps stood here and saw a stranger—someone he wanted to fight. Some days I think I see a stranger, too, but not tonight. Fortunately, it's just me, Jo Giordano, and I'm tired of fighting. I just want to fit in and have a good time.

I smile, checking to see that my teeth are clean and white—no poppy seeds. It feels good. Maybe Valerie's on to something after all. Maybe a little bit of self-love isn't a bad thing.

I pretend I'm Coach Granato, only I'm giving myself a pep talk for the dance and not a hockey game: "Go there tonight and have fun. Be confident. Talk to Ben. Write him that valentine if you want to." I start to giggle, remembering one more thing Coach always says: "And don't forget. There's no 'I' in 'team'!"

I jump when I hear a knock at the bathroom door.

"Who are you talking to in there, Jo?" Michael calls out.

I open the door and kneel down in front of him. "No one, buddy, I'm just getting ready for a dance."

"But, I heard you." Michael leans around me and cautiously inspects the bathroom floor.

Satisfied that I haven't dumped out the contents of the medicine cabinet, he places his small hands on either side of my face and narrows his eyes. "You look different, Jo-Jo," he says in a voice way too serious for a six-year-old.

"How?"

"Your eyelashes look like spider's legs and your lips are pink and shiny," he whispers.

I laugh. "It's only a little bit of makeup, silly."

"And your hair's all down and pretty," he says in his *Sesame Street* Cookie Monster voice.

I answer him as the Cookie Monster: "Thank you, Michael," and then hug and tickle him until he wriggles away from me, laughing and out of breath.

"Hey, you want to come to the dance?" I ask. "You want to be my date?"

"I don't wanna be a date," he says as he runs down the stairs. "I wanna drive the Zamboni when I grow up."

Outside in our driveway, Taryn's mom honks her horn. I grab my coat, kiss Mom and Michael good-bye, and head for the door.

"Jo," Mom calls after me, "don't underestimate the value of a good friendship."

I smile and nod.

Then, she whips the grunders out from behind her back and plops them on her head again. "Or the power of a fashion statement!"

Twelve

O ur gym is transformed, with strings of tiny white lights and large heart-shaped helium balloons floating everywhere. Even the glossy wood floor is covered in red confetti. Taped to the walls are the cheerleaders' construction-paper hearts, each with an individual message. Mixed in among them are pictures of famous celebrity couples.

Some of them I recognize from the old black-and-white movies Gramps and I used to watch together: Katharine Hepburn and Spencer Tracey, Lauren Bacall and Humphrey Bogart. If Ms. Freeman is here tonight, she'll be happy to see pictures of Cleopatra and Mark Antony, as well as Romeo and Juliet.

In the corner, a DJ spins records, while the teachers and parent chaperones pretend not to hear the words to the loud music. Principal Lubic, wearing a cupid tie, is at the door greeting everyone. "Have fun. Make smart choices!" he reminds us.

While Taryn's busy critiquing the decorations, I scan the gym, searching for Ben. I'm convinced that we'll finally talk to each other tonight, maybe even dance. And then everything will be as it was before.

Valerie's parading around as if she's prom queen, the rhinestone tiara back on her head from yesterday's *Caesar* debut.

Derek and some of his friends are dancing in the corner while a crowd gathers around. If Lubic sees the moves they're busting, he'd know they aren't taking his make-smart-choices speech very seriously.

No sign of Ben.

Maybe his father made him stay home to put a fifth coat of wax on the cars, or maybe he heard I was going to be here and decided to avoid the whole scene. At least he can't hide out in the library tonight.

"Taryn, I'm going to run to my locker. I forgot something." I might as well get the heart in case Ben shows up.

She waves and continues to sample the heart cookies on the table. "They sure stuck to the theme with this one."

As I hurry out the gym doors, I practically run into Ben, who is just arriving. I notice that his hair looks different—maybe he got it cut or put some gel in it. Also, he's wearing a new blue shirt that matches the color of his eyes. His shoulder is still in a sling.

"Jo!" he puts his good arm out to protect the injured side. He seems surprised and flustered to bump into me.

How embarrassing! Does he think I ran to the door to greet him or that I was waiting here ready to pounce? How desperate does that look?

"I was going to get something in my locker," I blurt out.

"Oh," he says with an awkward shrug. "I . . . I just got here."

116

Does he sound disappointed that I'm leaving? Or relieved?

"Nice decorations," I say, but he takes it like I'm being sarcastic, when I didn't mean it that way at all.

"I was just helping out," he says, irritated. "I can't play hockey and Valerie asked me to help."

Valerie! I don't want to hear her name tonight, especially from Ben. This is definitely not going the way I had hoped. Ben's not even in the door yet and he's mad at me, and I'm running away again! But now that I've said I'm going to my locker, I can't change my mind.

"Um, I'll be right back," I say, deciding to stick to my original plan of giving him the valentine.

"Sure." He shrugs.

"Where do you think you're going, Miss Giordano?"

Oh, no. It's Mr. Plotkin, looking serious, on hallway patrol outside the gym. I notice he doesn't have his bag-o-chalk tied to his belt and he's actually wearing jeans. It should be against the law for teachers to wear jeans. It makes them look like they're out of uniform, almost normal.

"Mr. Plotkin, I left my heart in my locker. I was going to get it."

"Why, you're in big trouble then. Are you sure you didn't leave it in San Francisco?" he chuckles at his goofy joke.

He's so weird.

"It's right down the hall. I'll only be a minute. I want to hang it up on the wall with the rest of the hearts." I lie. I have no intention of hanging it up for everyone to see.

"Let's get this straight," he says, tapping his fingers against his chin, which connects, turtlelike, to his neck. "You've got a lonely heart in your locker?" He pauses, clearly enjoying himself. "Hmm, guess that makes you a member of the lonely hearts club."

Ha, ha. Plotkin, the one-man comedy show. Unfortunately, I don't get any of his jokes. And at this rate, I'll never get back to the dance. I'll spend the entire evening trapped, listening to him tell every joke he can possibly think of pertaining to hearts.

What's next: heartache, heart and soul, heartburn? Which is exactly what he's giving me.

This calls for desperate measures.

Tilting my head to one side and wearing what I hope is a most persuasive smile, I say, "Please, Mr. Plotkin. It's really important."

I'm begging. No, it's worse than that. I am flirting with Plotkin. Gross!

Then a miracle. He extends his arm with a flourish, bowing ever so slightly at the waist, and says, "Proceed, Miss Giordano. And by the way, great game last week."

"Thank you!" I walk quickly down the hall before he changes his mind. I guess Plotkin's not so bad after all. Maybe he even knows a thing or two about a lonely heart.

Fortunately, my locker door springs open with a spin of the dial. I rummage through the chaos of books, papers, and chewed pencils that have recently begun to invade Taryn's artful design, but I can't find the hearts.

"Darn it! Taryn's right," I curse out loud. "Messy locker, messy life!"

I bought them two weeks ago and never wrote a message. I know I shoved them in here somewhere. I begin to search through my folders when suddenly I freeze. What is that noise?

There, again.

My heart races as I walk toward the sound. Here's one for Plotkin—heart attack.

I peer around the corner and see Angelo and Courtney sitting next to each other on the floor. Angelo leans over and whispers something in her ear.

Quickly, I turn away. There, two people "going out." No big deal. So what if they break up tomorrow and never speak to each other again. Live for the moment, right?

I stalk back to my locker and locate the paper hearts, which are stuck in my health folder—figures! Grabbing a pen, I'm determined to finally write something meaningful once and for all.

Brain freeze.

What should I write? A riddle? A threat: Meet me by the punch bowl in ten minutes or else!

Maybe the poem I wrote yesterday in Discover Tech. I take out the scrap of paper:

> *Friends since we were five,*
> *Now you don't know I'm alive.*
> *How can I make you see,*
> *Just what you mean to me.*
> *Let's start all over again,*
> *My best friend, Ben.*

"Pathetic!" I groan out loud, crushing it into a ball.

"Who's that?" Angelo calls from around the corner.

"It's Jo," I answer as I slump to the floor with my pen and crumpled heart in hand. "Trying to write a valentine."

"Well, get on with it!" he says.

Courtney giggles.

Angelo's right. Be decisive. Get on with it.

Reluctantly, I scribble some words on the heart, toss the pen back in, and then slam the locker door shut with such a terrific bang that it echoes up and down the hallway like the rumble of thunder.

There, I've made a decision.

Back in the gym, the dance floor's packed and it feels like a balmy ninety degrees. I can feel the beat of the music vibrating in my chest.

Lubic must have put an end to Derek's performance, because he and his gang are nowhere to be seen.

From across the dance floor, Taryn runs over to me. "Where have you been? You've got to read some of this crap on the wall!"

I check my pocket. No way am I taping Ben's heart up there for everyone to read. I'll just hand it to him in person, and whatever happens, at least I'll know I've tried to fix our friendship.

"There's one over here that I think you should read," Taryn says. She grabs my arm and pulls me across the gym to the far wall, where Mr. Gadlock and Lubic are busy ripping valentines down and stuffing them into garbage bags.

Derek stands there protesting, "Hey, I paid money for those. Whatever happened to free speech?"

"Young man, your right to free speech ends where my job to provide a safe, harassment-free educational environment begins!" bellows Lubic.

Gadlock backs him up, nodding his head up and down in agreement, like one of those bobble-head dogs my dad used to have on the dashboard of his truck.

"Censorship!" Derek shouts. "My father's an attorney!" From the smirk on Derek's face, you can tell that he's enjoying the entire scene.

"Inform your father that I'll be happy to meet with both of you first thing Monday morning so I can clarify school policy, since you've obviously neglected to read page twenty-three, section two-b, of the Student Handbook."

Derek snorts as Mr. Lubic walks away. He turns to his friends. "Yeah, hand this!" he says, grabbing his crotch.

They howl with laughter and pound him on the back.

"I think the boys have had enough sugar cookies for tonight," Taryn says.

"What did Derek's valentine say?" I ask.

"Oh, I don't know." She waves her hand at him dismissively. "Something about some hot substitute teacher." She grabs my sleeve to pull me along. "It's this one over here I want to show you."

Taryn's searching for a heart that's taped near the fire alarm, which is enclosed in a protective metal cage.

"Do you ever wonder how we're suppose to pull the alarm in an emergency?" I ask.

"Wire cutters?" Taryn shrugs. "Hey, look. There it is, that one right there." She hits me on the arm. "Read it."

"Stop it, Taryn! I can't read when you're poking me."

Taped in the middle of this heart is a small piece of white computer paper that says, *To Joanna G. Even when it rains, your sunshine remains. Love, B.M.*

I turn to Taryn and whisper, "Ben?"

"I told you he likes you." And she hits me in the arm for the third time. "Why don't you go find him? Ask him to dance."

"Stop it, Taryn. No more sugar for you, either."

"Come on, he's over there, by the dessert tables." She points to Ben. She gives me a little push. "Go ahead, get it over with."

I turn back to the poem and reread it. It's nice. And he did sign it, "Love, B.M."

"Okay, okay," I say, trying to disentangle myself from Taryn's insistent prodding. "Just stop pushing me!"

"Sometimes I don't get you, Jo." She's shaking her head angrily. "I mean, you're so fast and decisive on the ice, but off it—you're the queen of self-doubt. I swear if it helps, I'll go get you your helmet and stick and then you get your butt over there and talk to him."

"Why do you care? I feel like you're forcing me."

Taryn shrugs and tucks her hair behind her ears. "I don't know. I just do."

With one last push, she sends me on my way across the great divide of gym floor toward Ben McCloud, standing on the opposite side.

Deep breaths, I tell myself. I'll just thank him for his valentine and reach into my back pocket and give him the one I wrote for him. Now that I know how he feels, it'll be much easier. No problem . . . well, except maybe one. How do I really feel about him? I mean, I guess I've always thought about him in the best-friend, like-a-brother category.

It's not difficult to work my way toward Ben in the crowd—he's about a foot taller than everyone else standing around the tables and his auburn hair acts as a beacon.

I take one last deep breath and tap him on his good shoulder. "Hi, again."

"Hey, you're back." Trying to avoid jostling in the crowd, he shifts around so we're face-to-face.

Friends have signed the cloth sling that binds his shoulder to his chest. Some names I recognize from the team. An amazing fire-breathing dragon, drawn with colored markers, catches my attention as it snakes its way from Ben's forearm to his shoulder.

I point to it and ask, "Angelo?"

"Yeah, isn't it awesome?" Ben looks down, admiring the artwork.

I nod. "I saw him with Courtney earlier tonight. When I was at my locker . . . um, getting something."

Stalling, stalling—yawn!

I gulp one last deep breath. "Ben, I saw your poem hanging up over there." I point toward the far gym wall. "Thanks, I . . . I've been wanting to talk to you."

The expression on his face causes a logjam of words in my throat. And when Ben looks confused and says, "What poem?" everything crashes down into the pit of my stomach.

But I've gone too far to turn back, so I croak, "The one on the wall that says, 'Joanna G. Even when it rains, your sunshine remains.'"

Somehow, watching the uncomfortable look on his face, the words don't sound quite as beautiful and perfect as they did a moment ago.

"I didn't write that."

"You didn't? But they're your initials."

"Jo," he says so softly that I have to lean in closer to hear him over the loud music. "I'm no poet. Besides, I wouldn't—"

But he has no problem reading the embarrassed expression on my face, because he reaches for me with his good arm.

My throat tightens and I feel like my head is on fire. Quick! Somebody get the wire cutters and pull the fire alarm, while I go stick my head in the punch bowl.

"I'm such a dork!" I say out loud.

But humiliation is liberating, so I figure here's my chance to ask Ben why he's been acting so cold lately. Why he's basically dropped and slapped our friendship away like an old hockey puck. But I never get the chance before I'm practically knocked off my feet.

"Hey!" I shout as Derek and friends barrel into us.

They sing in high-pitched, helium-induced voices, "We represent the lollipop kids . . . we wish to welcome you to Munchkinland!"

Derek drapes his arm roughly over my shoulders.

"Cut it out!" I say, twisting free.

"Hey, Dorothy," Derek says, "who do you want to go out with? The Lion, Scarecrow, or Tin Man?"

"Knock it off, Derek." Ben stands taller and moves in. "We're talking."

"Oh, so you two are talking, now." Derek's voice loses all trace of helium, and he takes another hit from a balloon.

"*Excuuuse* me!" His voice rises with his friends' laughter.

I turn and walk away.

Unbelievable! I don't know if I'm shaking from relief that I avoided confronting Ben, or fury at Derek for butting in and preventing it.

Instantly, Taryn's at my side. "So, how did it go, Giordano? Mission accomplished?"

I groan and shake my head. "I'm a freak! I made a total idiot of myself! What does he think of me now?"

Taryn looks confused. "Did you tell him you saw his valentine?"

"Yes! But he says he didn't write it."

"What?" Taryn's mouth drops open. "Who did then?" she asks. "It's signed 'B.M.,' Ben McCloud. What other B.M. do we know?"

Then she gets this silly smile on her face.

"Don't go there. I'm in no mood," I warn her.

"Sorry, only trying to lighten things up a bit."

And then it hits me. "B.M., Brendan Mitchell, from Discover Tech! He sits right next to me in class." I bite my fingernail. "I should have known. He's always talking to me about hockey or computers."

"You mean *Mouse?* He actually talks? I don't think I've

heard him say two words ever. No wonder we didn't think of him," Taryn says.

"I know," I groan. "I guess I wanted it to be from Ben. . . ." I watch as Derek collides into another couple on the dance floor, but this time Lubic is all over him, shouting, "Strike three, young man!"

"I was going to give Ben a valentine I wrote for him."

"So, give it to him now," Taryn says, crossing her arms. "He's over there by the DJ."

"No, it's too late."

"Here," she holds out her hand. "I'll give it to him for you."

"No! He didn't write me one. I don't even know why I'm doing this. This valentine thing was all your idea, anyway."

"Duh, because you like him!" Taryn says.

"Yeah, I *like* him. But why now, all of a sudden, does that mean I have to go for boyfriend-girlfriend? When did the rules change?"

"That's the way it is, Jo. You're not a little kid anymore. Be your best f-r-i-e-n-d!" Taryn mimics.

"Shut up!"

"Whoa, you've got some negative energy going. How's your locker? Clutter-free, chimes still hanging?"

"No!" I glare at her.

"Hmm," she says. "Red paper?"

"Some," I mumble. "Most of it got jammed in the door and ripped and I couldn't get to my books for two days. Remember?"

Taryn tries to hide her smile behind her hand.

"It's not funny! You promised this fang shoe stuff would

flow through the locker and into my life. Order, harmony, happiness! *Hello?* I'm waiting."

"It's feng shui, and you made the hockey team, didn't you?"

"Yeah, *I* made the team because *I* went out there and skated my butt off! Got back on my feet every time I was knocked down and didn't let anyone stand in my way—not Derek, Lubic, Valerie, or even my own father!" I'm furious with Taryn right now. Always pushing me.

Taryn shrugs and says quietly, "Well, if you're not sure . . . if you're not going over there to tell him that you like him more than just a friend, then maybe I will."

"Oh, no, you won't! I asked you not to."

"You don't understand. Not for you, Jo—for me." She says this without meeting my eyes.

Now it's my jaw that's hanging open. "You! You like Ben? For how long?"

She nervously pushes her hair back behind both ears. "Well, for at least a couple of weeks now. I mean, I ... I think it started when we were rehearsing our lines for the play. We were both Roman citizens, you know, and we're—"

"I've liked him since kindergarten!" I practically scream at her, knowing even before the words leave my mouth how silly they sound.

"But, Jo," she grabs my arms, pleading with me. "You've proved it here tonight. You've had every opportunity. It's not like you like him like I do. Believe me, I wouldn't have said anything if I thought you cared for him more than that. It's just friends for you. That's it."

"That's not *it*, Taryn—at least not for me, it isn't." I jerk my arms free. "Friendship . . . friendship's everything!"

She stares at me, miserable and speechless, and I can see the tears welling up in her eyes. "I'm sorry," she whispers.

Damn! This is so not worth it. Everything is so mucked up and complicated. And what if I lose Taryn? I'll have no one.

"What I mean, Taryn, is you don't . . ." I pause, searching for the right words, feeling as if I'm teetering on the edge of a cliff.

And then suddenly it all seems perfectly clear and I make a decision. Taking a deep breath, I release it, and all the tension flows from my body. "Don't underestimate the value of a good friendship," I say.

Taryn nods in agreement, biting her lower lip so hard it looks painful.

Suddenly, I picture my mother sitting on the floor with underwear on her head. I smile and reach out for Taryn, scratching my hand on one of her funky metal earrings. "Ouch!" I say. "Or the power of a fashion statement!"

We hug each other, laughing with gratitude and relief.

Thirteen

Walking to the nursing home the next afternoon, I ask Mom if we can take the long way there, past St. Anthony's Church and school. When my dad's mother was alive, Dad used to take Jim and me to church with her every Sunday morning. I was only four or five years old and really don't remember much, except for the time I made my father proud.

During the offering, when the collection basket was passed around, Dad urged, "Put the money in the basket, Jo! In the basket!"

But no matter how hard he tried to pry open my chubby hands, I would not let go of the loose change. The Mass was being said in the school gym because the church roof leaked and was under repair. In that very same gym, I had watched probably fifty of Jim's CYO basketball games, and I knew darn well where the basket was.

The way Jim tells it, I just wound up and let 'em rip. Straight up into the air, I tossed my fistfuls of pennies toward the retracted hoops along the wall.

Coins clattered and rolled all over the wooden floor, the priest scowled, and the dearly devoted ducked or got nailed in the head. Jim remembers Dad beaming at the congregation in pride, his priorities clear, even back then.

"Did ya get a load of my kid's arm? Future hoop star, with a helluva sense of the basket!" he bragged to everyone within earshot.

We stopped attending soon after Grandma died. Maybe Dad was only going to make her happy anyway. There's nothing wrong with that, I guess. Still, I wouldn't mind that, if I decided to say a prayer once in a while, someone, somewhere out there, cared and was really listening.

It doesn't have to be God. I'm not one of those Jesus fanatics with a WWJD tourniquet wrapped around my wrist. Besides, I don't exactly have a personal relationship with him. Who I'd like it to be is Gram. I want to believe that she's watching over me still, cheering me on, sort of like my own spiritual fan club in the sky.

Who knows, maybe that's all heaven really is, anyway— our wish to remain close to people and animals we loved, despite the nuns insisting, "There're no pets in heaven!"

Which explains why I like visiting the nursing home on Sundays rather than going to church. Every Sunday, the local animal shelter brings pet carriers filled with rescued kittens and puppies so patients and visitors can cuddle the animals. Every once in a while, an abandoned animal gets lucky and is adopted by someone.

When I first started visiting on Sundays, I used to beg Mom for an orange kitten named Kitty. I spent hours holding her and listening to her purr in my arms. But Michael was allergic and there was no chance that Mom would give in to my tears.

Ben used to visit with me, too, sometimes. His father wouldn't permit him to have any pets because of the shedding, so Mom would take both of us on Sundays. Ben could play with the beloved golden retrievers he dreamed of owning, while I held Kitty.

Charlotte's not at the reception desk, so Mom and I sign ourselves in and head upstairs to see Gramps before playing with the animals in the commons room. The bird wind chimes are still hanging from the IV stand, and Gramps is sitting up in bed watching a televangelist.

The preacher claims to cure people's health problems by whacking them on the forehead with his hand. Supposedly, this chases the demons away, and then he spends the rest of the show selling his prayer cloths and books to the faithful viewers in TV land.

After a few minutes, I grab the remote and change the channel. I'm pretty sure no preacher's slap on the head is going to heal Gramps. And if I need a laugh, I'd rather watch Sunday-morning cartoons.

When I lean over to kiss Gramps on the cheek, I notice Mrs. Stritch's goose sitting on the floor in the corner of the room.

"Mom!" I point to it. "Did Gramps . . . ?"

She smiles. "No, Jo. Gramps hasn't been out of the nursing home. Mrs. Stritch came to visit the other day and gave the goose to him."

"What?" I can't believe what I'm hearing. Mrs. Stritch, who wanted Gramps to do hard time over this very same goose, suddenly decides to give it to him?

"She said that she's redecorating her front porch this spring and the goose doesn't fit with her new theme, so Gramps could have it."

"You're kidding."

"She's promised to visit now and then in order to change the goose's outfit," Mom says with a chuckle.

"It's not funny." I glare at the stupid plastic goose, which is still dressed in a felt Lincoln beard and stovepipe hat that's drooping somewhat with wear. "She's just looking for an excuse to stick her nose in our business!" I pick up the goose and shake it.

"What are you doing?"

"Checking for hidden microphones or recording devices."

Mom shakes her head. "It's not like that, Jo."

"Oh, yes it is," I insist. "Stritch-witch! That's what she is."

"You're being ridiculous," Mom says. She adjusts Gramps's covers and pours him a fresh glass of water from the pitcher on the nightstand beside his bed.

"Oh, yeah? Then why would Mrs. Stritch, the woman who terrorizes children and chases squirrels off her lawn . . . why would she give her precious goose to Gramps when he doesn't know the difference now between a goose and Godzilla?"

Mom snaps, "It's not for Gramps. It's for her. It gives her something to do, a place to go, a connection. She's lonely with no family. No one. Can't you give her a chance, Jo?"

I open my mouth to respond, but the words are all choked up inside. "I didn't know. I—" and then I remember all those garden statues, Mrs. Stritch's substitute family.

✳✳✳

When I enter the commons, the first thing I notice is the animal smell and a chorus of barking and meowing. The second thing is the tall guy with the auburn hair, standing next to Franny, holding a golden retriever pup in his arms.

I walk over to them immediately. "What are you doing here?"

"We didn't get a chance to talk last night." The puppy wriggles and twists in Ben's hands.

"Your sling is off. You going to play soon?"

"Yep, doctor thinks maybe this Friday. Hey, don't change the subject. About last night, I—"

"There's no problem. Forget it."

"Why won't you let me talk?" Ben demands. "You did the same thing the other day after practice."

"Let him talk, dear," Franny says as she gently tugs on my arm.

"Sorry, Franny." I squeeze her hand. "Ben, this is Franny Burton, Valerie's grandmother."

"Nice to meet you, Mrs. Burton," Ben says, leaning down to shake her hand.

Franny beams. "What a polite young man."

"Thanks," Ben says, but he looks flustered and quickly turns back to me. "No. No, actually I'm not polite, otherwise I would have apologized earlier. I wanted to make the team so badly, and then when I did, I just wanted . . . I guess, I wanted to fit in. I've never been with the popular crowd—Derek and all those guys. And they were all against you. They really hated you there for a while and I . . . I was afraid."

I reach out and pet the wriggling puppy without meeting Ben's eyes. "But we were friends," I say softly.

133

"I know. I . . . I guess I wasn't a very good one."

I take the pup from Ben, scratching behind its silky ears, holding it close to my face, smelling its sweet puppy breath. "I don't understand what you were afraid of. I mean, I was the one taking the abuse."

"I know. I can't explain it." Ben runs his hands through his hair and looks at me miserably. "It's like I wanted to stand by you, but then you'd get all fired up and go charging after something, like Derek, and that's not me. I'd just want to back away and lay low. That's the way I survive in my own house—avoiding my dad and any conflict."

I shrug my shoulders. "You know, I was jealous that you liked Valerie."

"I don't like Valerie." He shakes his head.

"Then I was jealous that Taryn liked you."

"Taryn likes me?"

"Yeah, she told me last night at the dance, but that's not the point. I finally figured out that I wasn't upset because I wanted to go out with you or anything. It wasn't like that. I just wanted you back. You were my best friend, Ben, and if you want to be friends again, well . . . you're just going to have to get some courage, moxie, chutzpah, balls, whatever you want to call it, because it really sucks to be dropped when things get tough."

My tears hit the pup's fur before I can blink them back. I hand the retriever to Ben and wipe my sleeve across my face. "I don't want to feel like that again. Friends stand by each other no matter what. It's just too hard any other way."

Ben shakes his head. "I know. I'm sorry, Jo."

"So." I give him a trembling smile. "Can you stay awhile and help pass out a few puppies?"

"Definitely," Ben says. "I remember coming here on Sundays, and I'm still an expert puppy-passer-outer. I think I've got a sixth sense or something for matching people and pets."

He gives Franny the golden retriever pup and it plays in her lap, biting the buttons on her expensive birthday sweater. She calls him "little rascal."

Franny looks up at us and says, "He's a keeper."

I hand Ben a sleepy calico kitten and he nestles it next to the baby doll in Rita's arms.

"Did you know Gramps is upstairs on three?" I ask.

"My mom told me what happened."

"He's okay. It's just that most of the time, I don't think he knows who I am anymore. He still looks like Gramps and his voice is the same, but his words don't have any connection to what's going on around him. It's weird because it's Gramps, but not really."

"Funny, because that's how I felt about myself lately. Like, I was Ben McCloud on the outside, but inside I was confused and just pretending like nothing was wrong."

"Gramps isn't pretending, and Michael doesn't understand why he can't come home."

"What's Michael up to?" Ben asks.

"You'll love this. Ever since he saw your arm in a sling, he's been practicing writing with his left hand, just in case he hurts his right. He still wants to be able to do his homework and drive the Zamboni."

Ben laughs. "I'll never forget last summer, when he called time-outs for the Zamboni during our street hockey games, and then he'd ride around on his bicycle dragging a soaking-wet towel tied to the back, pretending to clean the ice."

"Favorite part of the game," I laugh.

"How's your dad?" Ben asks.

"Busy. Taking some classes—anger management. He's banned from attending any more hockey games this season."

"That's too bad."

"It's okay. At least he's trying. And your dad? Still, washin' and waxin' the cars?"

He laughs and plays tug-of-war with a rolled-up newspaper and a female Shepherd mix. "Hey, do you think Gramps would like to hold a puppy?"

I scoop the pup up into my arms and she yelps in protest. "Come on, let's go up and give it a try."

The elevator door opens. Empty this time. No bridal procession parading through today. I push the button for three, and we feel the floor lift beneath us.

Ben strokes the pup's head, and it nips playfully at his hand. "Thanks, Jo," he says.

"What are you thanking me for?"

"I don't know. For a second chance?"

"Hey!" I laugh as the pup chews and gets her paws caught in my curly hair.

Ben reaches over and tries to help untangle us.

"Everyone deserves a second chance," I say.

GOFISH

DAWN FITZGERALD

What did you want to be when you grew up?
When I was in kindergarten, I wanted to be a firefighter because I liked the idea of saving people.

When did you realize you wanted to be a writer?
Since I was a little girl, I've always kept a journal. In college, I was an English major and eventually became a teacher. Always in the back of my mind I'd dreamed of writing a children's book. I didn't actually believe I could do it until I was in my thirties, sitting in school assemblies listening to authors tell their stories and feeling like, hey, maybe this could be me!

What's your first childhood memory?
I was three or four, watching older kids playing in the back-yard of a duplex we lived in on Central Avenue in Yonkers, New York.

What's your most embarrassing childhood memory?
In kindergarten, there was a bulletin board at school and you had to memorize and recite your address in front of the class to get a roof on your construction-paper house pinned to the

board. I was one of the last kids to get a roof. I had to sing my address in order to remember it.

As a young person, who did you look up to most?
My mother. Everyone thought my mother with her long, blonde hair looked like Cinderella.

What was your worst subject in school?
High school physics! My teacher used to hold out a pass, joking that he would send me to home economics class, where I belonged.

What was your first job?
Babysitting my four younger siblings and the neighborhood kids for one dollar an hour.

How did you celebrate publishing your first book?
Ordered pizza!

Where do you write your books?
I use a laptop and need to have earplugs in my ears and then I can write anywhere.

Where do you find inspiration for your writing?
My childhood experiences, magazine and newspaper articles, my own two children, and the students I teach.

Which of your characters are most like you?
The feisty ones.

When you finish a book, who reads it first?
My twelve-year-old daughter is the best critic and fan.

Are you a morning person or a night owl?
Morning person—but if I'm reading a good book, I've been known to stay up until 2 a.m.

What's your idea of the best meal ever?
Anything my mom makes. Italian food is her specialty.

Which do you like better: cats or dogs?
Unfortunately, I'm allergic to both, but I love animals—dogs and cats equally.

What do you value most in your friends?
Sense of humor, thoughtfulness.

Where do you go for peace and quiet?
To the library! But with earplugs, you can pretty much have quiet anywhere.

What makes you laugh out loud?
Funny things my children or students say.

What's your favorite song?
"Come On, Get Happy"—The Partridge Family.

Who are your favorite fictional characters?
Scout Finch: *To Kill a Mockingbird*, and Lyra Belacqua: *The Golden Compass* (His Dark Materials Trilogy).

What are you most afraid of?
Losing the people I love.

What time of the year do you like best?
Autumn—new beginnings at school. The sights and smells of fall leaves.

What is your favorite TV show?
The Office.

If you were stranded on a desert island, who would you want for company?
My family and hundreds of books.

SQUARE FISH

If you could travel in time, where would you go?
Women's suffrage movement of the early twentieth century.

What's the best advice you have ever received about writing?
Persistence, practice, patience.

What do you want readers to remember about your books?
Humorous, feisty characters that have the courage to pursue their dreams!

What would you do if you ever stopped writing?
Voice-recognition software.

What do you like best about yourself?
Caring. Creative. Curious.

What is your worst habit?
Hiding stashes of chocolate around the house.

What do you consider to be your greatest accomplishment?
Raising two kind, intelligent, hardworking kids.

What do you wish you could do better?
Budget my time for all that I want and need to accomplish.

What would your readers be most surprised to learn about you?
I talk the dialogue to my stories out loud as I'm writing and rewriting, and my talking pet parakeet, Boo, thinks that I'm teaching him new words.

SQUARE FISH